From ***A Clean Kill*** by M. E. Cooper –

The corpse was found when a maid opened a door with a *Do Not Disturb* sign on it and started screaming.

Vic responded quickly, ordering everyone not to touch anything. He called immediately to Homicide, his old department.

In short order, the officers responded, but after a while, one of the new homicide detectives named Bert Riley called him over, asking, "What made you think it was a murder?"

For Amy,
who also likes animals,
Marion Moore Hill

Almostly Murder…

…With Pets

An Anthology of Mystery Short Stories
by
The Cozy Crime Writers

Deborah Bouziden
M. E. Cooper
Audrey Eggers
Rey Hanan
Marion Moore Hill
Sara Sue Hoklotubbe
Sharon K. Hudgins
Judith Sexton
Moira K. Wiley

This is a work of fiction. All the characters and events portrayed in this book are either products of the authors' imagination or are used fictionally.

ALMOSTLY MURDER... WITH PETS

Art by Audrey Eggers

Published by:
Padlock Mystery
412 East Ninth
Stillwater, Oklahoma 74074

www.mecooper.com

ISBN: 0-9662020-7-4

First edition: November 2002

Printed in the United States of America

Editor's Note

by Audrey Eggers

As a member of a critique group, I have read a large number of excellent manuscripts that have never been available in the marketplace. Short stories especially have a very limited market, and yet this American art form aptly fits our national lifestyle. They are concise, distracting, time saving, and – well – short.

Some of these stories were written especially for this anthology. Some have resided in file cabinets and on computer disks for years. Here we are proud to give them the light of day and the readership they deserve.

The writers are serious about their craft, all of them members of Oklahoma Writers' Federation, Inc. (OWFI). Many of them are members of other groups: Sisters in Crime, the National League of American Pen Women, Mystery Writers of America, National Association of Women Writers, Wordcraft Circle of Native American Writers and Storytellers, Stillwater Writers, Red River Writers, Cimarron Valley Writers, Central Oklahoma Roundtable of Authors, Oklahoma Mystery Writers.

As for that word *Almostly* – it's a play on words. And The Cozy Crime Writers do love to play with words.

Acknowledgements

To all the writers who joined this project with such enthusiasm, talent and professionalism, thank you.

To the members of Stillwater Writers who have helped writers develop their craft and have encouraged writers to spread their wings, we appreciate you.

To Oklahoma Writers Federation, Inc. for the conferences, contests, newsletter and for the affirmation that it pays to keep on trying, we salute you. Sometimes the pay is actual money. And sometimes the pay, at least for a while, is the satisfaction of developing as a writer and sharing time with others who dream our dreams and talk our talk.

To family members who have supported and encouraged along the way, we love you.

Introduction

by M. E. Cooper

The short stories here combine mystery and pets.

All of us are Oklahoma writers who love our furry and feathered friends, whether feline, canine, fowl or even reptiles. We each owe a debt of gratitude to our friendly veterinarians (in addition to our vet bills, of course).

Seriously, the ladies of the Cozy Crime Writers are as different as our stories. Moira K. Wiley is a whirlwind of activity, whether chasing tornadoes or runaway emus. Sara Sue Hoklotubbe finds her country home near Tahlequah enhanced by her dogs.

While Marion Moore Hill has both cats and dogs near her home in Durant, Stillwater residents, Rachelle "Rey" Hanan, M. E. Cooper and Judith Sexton all share a love for dogs. Sharon K. Hudgins of Cushing favors exotic animals, but Audrey Eggers of Morrison has more prosaic tastes for cats that frolic in the barn near her farmhouse. Deborah Bouziden, when not genealogy hunting, shares her Edmond home with both cats and dogs.

Most of our stories would be considered 'cozy.' However, there are a few that may cause the reader to feel a chill. That's enough introduction. Turn the page and enjoy!

Almostly Murder … With Pets
An Anthology of Mystery Short Stories

Table of Contents

M. E. Cooper writes contemporary cozies, true crime and historical mysteries set in the Civil War and Renaissance Italy. She was nonfiction guest of honor at Cluefest in 2001 and is a popular speaker at conferences, libraries and writing groups – especially when she transforms herself into a 15th century lady locksmith. Even a fleeting idea spins into a mystery plot at her hands, and she is as relentless as a bloodhound at the mere sniff of an intriguing snippet of a clue.

~

A Clean Kill

by M. E. Cooper

The night manager insisted on being called Mr. Hartley, but Vic privately referred to him as the Kid, because he appeared younger than his own grown sons. Vic really didn't appreciate the condescending, patronizing tone the Kid used when talking to him. Then he reminded himself, his family hadn't wanted him to take this job.

Vic Junior had said, "I know it's lonesome for you in this big house with Mom gone, but why do you need to work? Why can't you fish or play golf or something?"

"I never liked to fish. Golf isn't my game, so what's wrong with me working?"

Sally, his youngest, had said, "Daddy, you'll be bored. After all those years on the force investigating homicides, to be a security guard in a hotel? I don't think you'll like it."

He had hugged her and told them all to quit worrying

about him. But now he wondered if they might be right. Mr. Hartley was instructing him about things he'd learned years ago in the Academy. He resisted yawning. Finally, he was told to go about his duties. He smiled cheerfully at the Kid, just to get his goat, because he suspected the feelings of animosity were mutual.

"Oh, Vic, I forgot to mention. You're responsible for the mutt."

"What?" Vic looked down at the small dog who cocked his head at him. Not much bigger than a Chihuahua, the animal had an intelligent look in her eyes that immediately charmed Vic, but he didn't want to show it.

"Why do I have to babysit the dog?"

"Of course, if you'd rather resign?" Hartley's voice was silky, inviting the older man to take the bait.

"No, that's all right. I've always liked dogs," Vic said, remembering his own German Shepherds and Black Labs. "What's the dog's name?"

Harley smirked. "Fergie. Named for the former Duchess of York. This scroungy canine is supposed to be a Yorkshire Terrier or terror, more like it. If the owner of this chain of hotels didn't insist, the mutt would be taken to the pound."

"C'mon, Fergie." As he walked down the spacious halls, he noticed that the dog was well trained and seemed to follow him naturally.

An uneventful week went by and Vic felt he was getting to understand the way the hotel was run and what he could expect. Then he opened a door, followed by Fergie, when the dog went berserk. Barking and jumping up and down, Fergie led him to a bathroom, where Vic saw what he assumed was a big inflatable toy in the bathtub.

"College students!" He sighed, then chuckled. The beach toy looked almost real. Then it opened its mouth and Vic jumped back, startled.

"By damn, it's a real alligator!" With one hand, he put

Fergie in a closet, while with the other he grabbed his cell phone, dialing animal control. "What do you mean you don't do alligators? It's an animal and you're animal control!"

He listened for a moment and then hung up, immediately dialing another number.

"We got a nuisance alligator in a hotel bathtub. How soon can you get here to get it?"

He listened intently, shaking his head at the "good ole" boy tone of the fellow on the other end. "You're tied up all day. What am I supposed to do?"

He listened awhile longer. "All I need is to drop a noose over the jaws and use duct tape? Just keep the mouth closed until I get it taped and watch out for the tail? You sure about that?"

He listened for a while longer, than shook his head in amazement.

With assistance from the hotel maintenance men, he managed to remove the alligator.

Later, he was soothing the little dog. "Sorry, Fergie, but I couldn't take the chance you'd end up a snack for that alligator." Vic smiled to himself. He hadn't decided if he'd tell his grown kids about the excitement today or not. They both tended to be over protective of him and so far, he liked his job as hotel security.

Two weeks had gone by with no surprises, and then a corpse was found. A maid opened a door with a *Do Not Disturb* sign on it and started screaming.

Vic responded quickly, ordering everyone not to touch anything. He called immediately to Homicide, his old department.

In short order, the officers responded, but after a while, one of the new homicide detectives named Bert Riley called him over, asking, "What made you think it was a murder?"

"Well, I didn't study the body, but from what I saw of

the corpse he was a young guy wasn't he?"

"His driver's license says 41 years old."

"Yeah. A young guy."

Bert raised his eyebrows and Vic realized that what looked young to a 65 year old didn't look so young for a detective in his early thirties.

"You tellin' me this was a natural causes death?"

Bert shrugged. "The Medical Examiner will get the body. Maybe he'll have some answers. There's no wounds on the body, no appearance of trauma. Looks like the guy just died in his sleep."

Vic watched them wheel the body out and thought for a while. Then he went to the front desk. "The dead guy, what was his name?"

"Rhett Beauregard."

"Sounds like a fine southern gentleman. Did he come here often?"

"Pretty often. He was a salesman. You know something that always struck me a little funny about him is that he lives right here in town, but he says he likes to relax here before he goes home."

"Really?" Vic stroked his chin, thinking. Most of the salesmen he knew took traveling as just part of the job, but once they got close to home, they were ready to hit the sheets in their own bed, not stay in some hotel, even a nice one. "Did he ever check in with a lady?"

The desk clerk smirked. "You think he was getting a little on the side?"

"Well, he sure ain't any more," Vic said as he strode away.

Since the forensic team had finished in the death room, Vic went in and looked around. Fergie had followed him, and she was sniffing everywhere, looking up at him with that bright curious expression on her little face.

"Everything seems clean and sanitary. Almost too sanitary." He sniffed the air. Seeing a maid in the hall, he motioned to her.

"This room smells funny."

"It is not dirty." The maid glared at him.

"No, no, I don't mean dirty, it just smells funny. Like some kind of cleaning stuff or something."

"It is clean." She glared at him.

Fergie was sniffing around and then she pawed at the machine near the maid, barking several times to get Vic's attention.

"What's that? Some new kind of vacuum cleaner?"

"Oh. That's the ozone machine."

"Ozone machine?"

"Yes. After a whiskey spill, or cigar smokers, something like that, we have to put the ozone machine in a room for several hours. It draws the smell out."

"Can you show me how this machine works?"

"Of course. You just plug it in and leave it running for several hours while the room is vacant."

Vic examined the machine, studying the warning label on the side with interest. Fergie licked his hand, as giving her approval.

A few days later, Vic called the Homicide department and asked for Bert. "What did the medical examiner say about our dead salesman?"

"It's a strange thing, Vic. The M.E. says the guy had some booze in him and a few sleeping pills, but not enough to kill him. He appears to have just quit breathing, but the M.E. can find no cause for it."

"Can you give me the victim's wife's name and address? I'd like to call on her, if you don't mind."

"Be my guest." Bert rattled off the information.

Vic had no trouble finding the address. He walked up to the ranch style house and rapped on the door.

"Are you Alice Beauregard?"

"Yes."

She looked wary when he flashed his badge at her. It

was his old badge, but he didn't tell her that, and she let him inside.

"What is it officer? Why are you here?"

"It's about your husband's death." When she looked at him steadily, he played a hunch. "I've seen you before, you know."

"You have?"

"Yes. When you were wearing a maid's uniform and wheeling the ozone machine down the hall. Of course, I didn't realize at the time that you were going to kill him with it."

She paled, staggered a moment, and then sat down, putting her face in her hands, sobbing. "I knew someone would find out. I knew I couldn't get away with it."

"Why did you do it then?"

"Because he cheated on me all the time. He didn't care! He took his floozies to that hotel, and then he would come home to me. I hated him!" She commenced sobbing again.

"Tell me one thing. Where did you get the uniform? And where did you get the idea of using the ozone machine?"

"My sister got the uniform for me. She works in another hotel, and she told me how dangerous the ozone machines are. They suck all the oxygen out of a room."

Vic said, "I'm going to use your phone now." He called Bert in Homicide and told him the victim's wife had just confessed to killing her husband. Bert was properly grateful. After Vic watched her taken off in handcuffs, he walked thoughtfully back to his own car.

When he got to the hotel, Mr. Hartley, the Kid, looked at the clock and sneered, "You're an hour early for your shift. What's the matter, can't you find anything else to do?"

"Oh, this job's not so bad at all. In fact, it can get down right interesting." Fergie jumped up and barked, and Vic thought she was smiling.

A ***Marion Moore Hill***, author of *Bookmarked for Murder*, has an astute ear for dialogue and a strong sense of place in her writing. Her connection to the other writers is one of friendship sustained through email and attendance at conferences. She is an adult literacy tutor and formerly tutored English as a Second Language in Durant, Oklahoma, the home of Southeastern Oklahoma State University. Marion always orders dessert, although you could never tell it by looking.

~

Bear With Me

by Marion Moore Hill

"Oh, Bear!"

The woolly black puppy sat back on his haunches, regarding Allison with a placid, tongue-dangling expression. Grains of dirt spilled from his wide muzzle.

"Kevin and I worked so hard on this lawn," she wailed. Setting down her briefcase and purse, she grabbed his collar and scolded, "Bad dog! I'm going to kill your owner when she gets home."

He shut his mouth and cocked his head, looking so quizzical Allison had to chuckle.

"Sure made a mess of your front yard, didn't he?" a frail voice spoke nearby.

"Oh, hi, Ridley," Allison said.

Her neighbor, a stooped, gray-haired man with a gentle, lined face and a hangdog manner, stood looking over the high wooden fence separating their properties. She walked over.

"You know anything about training dogs?" she asked plaintively. "My co-worker Karen was given this one as a gift, and she left for Europe with her parents soon after. I don't know how to make an animal behave--especially a big, unruly puppy like Bear."

Hearing his name, the dog waved his white-tipped tail, brushing the turf behind him. Liquid dark eyes regarded the humans with good will.

"We've allus had cats," murmured Ridley. "Leastways my wife did. My daughter won't have *any* pets around."

Hearing wistfulness in his voice, Allison asked, "Carolee hasn't moved back home yet?"

"Nah. Her and her husband's still having problems." He sighed. "I wish—"

"Dad! What you doing out there so long?"

Ridley cringed, turned to look at the petite blonde on the porch behind him. "Nothing much. Just passing the time of day with Miss Williams."

Allison waved a hello. Carolee glared, whipped around, strode into the house and banged the door. Allison raised an eyebrow.

"She don't like me having friends," Ridley confided. "Especially women. But lord, Allison, Margaret's been dead nigh five years."

"Is Carolee afraid you'll remarry?"

"I guess. Not that I have much to leave her anyway. Only this house."

Allison glanced over his tidy bungalow and well-kept grounds. "It's a nice place." She noticed a spindly bush sticking out of newly turned earth at the rear corner of his dwelling. "Oh, you've planted something new. Seems late to put out roses, but you probably know more than I do about gardening."

He smiled sheepishly. "I set it out while Carolee was at her bridge club last night. She give me 'what for' this morning for planting it late, putting it so close to the house, mostly for not checking with her first. A friend give it to me the other day, and I couldn't say no."

"A woman friend?" Allison couldn't resist teasing.

He colored. "Yeah, but it ain't like — that. Her and her *husband* goes to my church. We're all in the same Sunday school class."

"Just kidding, Ridley. You have a right to any friend you choose, either sex."

He smiled slyly. "Who knows? Maybe I will get hitched again some day."

A blue Ford approached, turned into Allison's drive and stopped. Her heart quickened. Kevin had said he wouldn't be over today, had too much to do, yet here he was.

The tall, dark-haired man in policeman's garb got out. Bear galloped over to him, nuzzled his leg and sniffed at the two paper bags he carried, each bearing an "Imperial Gardens" logo.

"Chow time," Kevin said. "Evening, Mr. Jessup."

"How'd you know it was a hellacious day at work?" Allison said as she hugged him. "And that I came home to *this*!" She pointed to the excavation.

He kissed her. "Figured we could at least eat together if I got takeout." Kevin scratched the dog's ears and nodded toward the pile of dirt. "Bear was probably trying to beat the heat – soil's cooler a few inches down."

"It is awfully hot, for April."

"And he's still wearing his winter coat. Maybe I could fill that hole in tomorrow. I'll have more time then."

"Thanks, but I can do it." She wouldn't be the sort who always wanted something from him, she vowed. Not like

Marsha must've been ....

Allison gave the dog a stern look. "Bear's digging isn't the only problem. He's also a thief. Yesterday I caught him with somebody's outdoor-furniture cushion. I went around knocking on doors and finally learned it belonged to the Brierses. They sometimes leave their garage door open, and he must've gone in and helped himself."

"Well, the city ordinance on pets doesn't apply this far out, but I suggest you either tie him or pen him up." Kevin's cheerful, homely face smiled broadly. "Bear keeps this up, he'll get you run out of the neighborhood."

Allison grimaced. "I hate the thought of tying him, Kev. Bear's a nuisance but a sweetheart. Such a good-natured dog."

"Maybe that fence in back could be fixed good enough to keep him in. We'd better eat—I promised to help Theo with a school project before my shift. See you, Mr. Jessup."

Allison and Kevin hurried into the house so he had time for his nephew's project. While he set out their supper, she freshened the dog's water and food bowls near the back door. She looked around her yard, bounded on three sides by tall, dense bushes. Kevin was right. A secure pen could be made by repairing the decrepit wooden fence and the gates opening into Ridley's yard and the alley behind both homes. But her attempts at carpentry usually led to smashed thumbs. And Kevin hadn't offered, nor did she feel she could ask at this point in their relationship.

They ate at a table in her sunny yellow kitchen, half listening to the evening news on a television set on the counter.

"Bad day at work, huh?" Kevin said around a mouthful of Szechwan shrimp.

"Brutal. The other loan officer's out sick, and half of Oklahoma was in the bank today applying for mortgages."

"We're short-handed too. I see double shifts in my

future."

A dancing roll of paper towels on TV faded, and a well coiffed young man holding a microphone appeared. A sign on the building behind him said "Tulsa Police Department."

"Speaking of work..." Kevin said with a rueful grin.

"Police are investigating an anonymous phone tip received by KTUL-TV," the reporter said, "which claimed that foul play was involved in the Monday disappearance of Mrs. Willa Sloan. According to the male caller, and I'm quoting now: 'Jacob Sloan knows a lot more than he's telling about what happened to his wife.'"

File footage of the missing woman replaced the newsman's image, while his voice recapped an earlier report: Mrs. Sloan had been scheduled to speak at a charity luncheon two days ago. When she didn't show up, the event's organizer called her law partner, learning only that she had left work before noon to go to the luncheon.

The TV picture showed an auburn-haired beauty chatting with two well-dressed older men at a reception for a visiting dignitary, her manner genteel but lively, bordering on flirtatious. She wore a stylish navy dress set off by a silver *S*-shaped pendant and a flashy two-carat diamond ring.

The scene changed to a shot of her husband, a stockbroker, being interviewed by a female reporter the previous Monday.

"I'm absolutely distraught," Jacob Sloan said, the balding, baggy-eyed man's morose expression at odds with his passionate words. "We talked about the luncheon this morning, and I've no reason to think Willa had changed her plans. Obviously I'll be filing a missing-persons report on her."

The live picture reappeared, again showing the reporter in front of the police station. "Jacob Sloan said today through a spokesman that the phone call is obviously a cruel hoax, intended to hamper police in their quest to learn what really happened to his wife."

"Didn't you say the Sloans live near you?" Kevin asked.

Allison nodded. "That big Dutch Colonial two doors down. I only know her to speak to, but she seems friendly enough. I sometimes see her visiting with Ridley over the fence between their yards."

"Attractive woman."

"She is. Not pretentious, either. Their house is the nicest in the neighborhood—not that there's any zoning out here—but it's no mansion. And she isn't much for jewelry except for her wedding rings."

"Her husband looks kinda stodgy."

"Mm. It's my impression he's wrapped up in his work. She often goes out evenings, but he's never with her."

"Maybe she ran away from home to find some excitement."

"Possibly. Be an odd way to leave, though, wouldn't it?"

He shrugged. "You oughta see some of the stuff I see. Domestic disputes – they're the worst."

He finished eating, kissed Allison goodbye and left. She cleaned up the few dishes, thinking as she did so about their weeks-old courtship. Kevin seemed genuinely fond of her but never referred to a future together. He seldom even made a date more than a couple of days ahead. She knew he had been hurt when his former girlfriend broke off with him, though from the little he had said, Marsha sounded unworthy of him.

Allison knew about bad breakups. But it had been over a year since she and Charlie had called it quits; Kevin's pain was fresher. She wouldn't push, Allison resolved. If a long-term commitment worked out, great. If not…she didn't want to think about that.

Changing to an old tee shirt and shorts, she went back outside to fill in the hole. Bear "helped," nosing and scratching at the shovel as it moved between dirt pile and cavity. Finally, she got a length of rope and fastened him to the front doorknob. He wriggled, tugged at his tether and barked his unhappiness.

"That's just a sample, if you keep up your nonsense." But as soon as she'd finished her chore, she released him and watched as he capered joyfully over the lawn.

The next day, the *Tulsa World* reported the arrest of Jacob Sloan for the murder of his wife. Incriminating evidence had been found at and near their home, the newspaper said, including a bloody handkerchief in a dumpster in the back alley – blood that had proved to be Mrs. Sloan's. The receptacle got emptied weekly, the last time on the previous Friday.

"This is an outrage," the *World* quoted Sloan's attorney as saying. "My client is an honest, hard-working businessman who has no idea what became of his wife.

"He certainly didn't harm her in any way, and he's devastated over her disappearance."

That evening, as Allison weeded a bed of sweet peas near her back door, Bear tied to a redbud tree centering the yard, she looked up to see Ridley's head and shoulders above their common fence.

"Say, there, Allison," he said softly.

"Ridley." She got to her feet, brushed off the knees of her jeans and joined him. "How's everything going?"

"Well…I think your dog – your friend's dog – musta carried off my gardening shoe."

"Oh? I haven't seen one anywhere around."

"Well, I don't know what else coulda got it. I set them both right outside my back door yesterday."

"I'll look when I finish up here. By the way, what do you think about Mr. Sloan's arrest? Suppose he really did murder his wife?"

"I—" Ridley looked at the ground and swallowed hard. "Cain't see nobody killing Mrs. Sloan. She's a real nice lady."

"But if she wasn't murdered, what do you think happened? Suppose she left of her own free will?"

He blinked rapidly three times. "Dunno." As if suddenly remembering something, he cleared his throat and added, "I guess if anybody did—kill her, he'd be as likely as anybody to of did it."

"So you do think it's possible. Was she afraid of him? Did she tell you they were having trouble?"

He blushed. "She wouldn't say, even if they was. She was a *lady*."

"I didn't mean to imply she wasn't. Well, I'd better finish my weeding before dark. Nice talking to you, Ridley. I sure hope your friend, Mrs. Sloan, is okay. And I'll keep an eye out for your shoe."

She completed her task and untied Bear, who cavorted beside her as she walked all around her property. She found the missing footwear in the back yard, under a bush near the alley gate. She held the slipper in front of Bear, shook her finger and tried to sound menacing.

"Bad dog! *Bad* dog!"

He licked at the shoe as if it were a treat she was offering and looked questioningly at her. Seeing his innocent bewilderment, she dissolved in laughter.

"Oh, Bear," she said, wiping her eyes, "you irritating, impossible, lovable beast, you."

He nosed her shoulder, rear end waggling, eyes shining as if with joy at the new game they had invented.

Saturday, Kevin surprised her again, showing up with

tools and supplies to work on her fence. He put in several hours replacing decrepit uprights, securing loose boards and repairing gates.

"There," he said as he flopped onto her back stoop in late afternoon, tossed down his hammer and wiped sweat from his forehead. "Let's see the young man get out of that."

"Wonderful, Kevin. Thanks." She handed him a glass of iced tea, sipped another and sat beside him. "Uh, you don't suppose he'll be able to jump over the fence?"

"Shouldn't think so. If he does...well...I guess you'll have to build it up higher. That, or tie him."

"Right." Keeping her voice light, she said, "You're a nice guy, Kev. You work hard at your job, help your nephews with their homework and still find time to do things around here."

"Just a softy, I guess." He kissed the tip of her nose, his manly scent blending with the fragrance of sweet alyssum beside the steps. Bear watched lazily from under the redbud.

"Sorry to cramp your style, old fellow," Kevin told him, "but this'll be better. The way you were roaming the neighborhood, you might've gotten hit by a car." He turned to Allison. "How about celebrating the success of the fence project with Valentino's and a flick?"

"You're on."

He went home to shower, change and feed his own animals – three cats and an elderly dog – while she got ready and checked the movie ads. When he returned, they left Bear chasing a robin inside his mended enclosure and drove to Allison's favorite Italian restaurant. After an enjoyable meal, followed by a French farce that further lightened her mood, she invited him in for coffee. They carried full cups outside to admire Kevin's handiwork and learn how Bear was adapting.

Allison didn't see him anywhere.

"Bear!" she called.

A low whine came from the direction of the board fence. She strained to see beyond the porch light's glow.

"Spotting a black dog at night isn't easy," she said wryly. "Bear! Where'd you go?!"

This time a bark sounded near Ridley's house.

"That sounds like him. Where in the—"

Kevin had switched on the flashlight he always carried and was shining it over the fence.

"There he is. In Ridley's yard." He glanced down, near his own feet. "Son of a gun! He dug his way out, *under* the fence!"

"Oh, Kev," Allison groaned. "After all your hard work…."

"Should've figured that as a possibility, I guess. Hold on a sec. Bear seems to've found something over there. Something shiny." He opened the gate and stepped through, Allison right behind him.

"We should let Ridley know we're over here," she muttered. "It's not very nice to—" She broke off as Kevin picked up the object and shone the torch full on it.

A long, narrow *S* glittered up at her.

"Mrs. Sloan's necklace," Allison breathed. "What's it doing here?"

Kevin waved the light over a dirt pile, a hole and a scrawny rosebush. Allison felt her heart sink.

"Oh…" she said. "Oh…Ridley…."

Kevin unhooked his cell phone from his belt and dialed his work number.

Bear wagged his entire rear end, clearly proud of his find. Allison dropped to her knees and buried her face in his fur. As if he sensed her sadness, his tail slowed and his nose pressed against her neck.

Ridley Jessup sat straight, almost regally, in the interrogation-room chair, facing two unsmiling detectives across a table. His hands shook, his eyes seldom met theirs, but a touch of the aristocrat clung to him as he courteously responded to questions.

When had he last seen or talked with Mrs. Sloan?

Last Saturday. Or maybe Sunday.

What had they talked about?

The usual: whether it would rain as promised by the TV weatherman, the high price of gasoline. The usual.

What was his relationship with her?

A hesitation. Then, just friends.

Friends. Strange, wasn't it? Why had she picked him for a "friend"?

She seemed lonely.

Lonely? A woman like her, beautiful, successful, respected in the community? Lonely?

No response. The barrage continued, picking away at the oddity of the tale. A woman who had everything, and her elderly neighbor, who must have watched her from afar, maybe had his advances politely rebuffed. Obsessed with what he couldn't have, Ridley had killed her.

"No!" Ridley cried in horror, his courtly air gone. "I wouldn't do no such thing. We're – was – are – friends. Anyway, I'm not like that."

"Then how'd you happen to have her necklace?"

"She give it to me."

"Oh, yeah? Pretty fancy present. Why'd you bury it under a bush? At night?"

Ridley visibly wilted, laid his forearms on the table and hid his face against them.

"Cain't take no more," he quavered. "I promised her…but I just cain't…."

"Promised who?"

"Willa – Mrs. Sloan. She wanted – just wanted to live a

better life somewheres else. I tried to help her...."

The story spilled out. Mrs. Sloan had conceived a scheme to disappear and frame her despised husband for her murder. She would disguise her appearance, live somewhere in the area – she hadn't told Ridley where – and watch events play out in the Tulsa media before moving on. She had sent deposits over time to an out-of-town bank under an assumed name, awaiting the right opportunity to carry out her plan.

Ridley had thought it a joke at first, then had tried to talk her out of it. But she had complained so about her boring life, had begged Ridley to be the gallant man she knew he was and help her in her distress. At last, he had agreed.

She herself had planted the bloody handkerchief in the trash. The *S* pendant had been a going-away and thank-you gift to Ridley. With his daughter around, he had been afraid to keep the jewelry in the house, so he had buried it, planning to retrieve it once Carolee had gone.

Reluctantly, he told authorities all the places Willa Sloan had ever mentioned. It wasn't long before she was found and brought back to face charges, along with the lover who had called in the tip to the television station for her.

Karen returned from abroad, flouncing forth from her red Camry with complaints about the inconvenience of having a dog. Bear, released by Allison from his confining rope, greeted his owner with a half-hearted tail-wag.

"Jason didn't even ask if I wanted a dog before presenting this one to me," Karen said, tossing her platinum hair. "And when I dumped Jason, he refused to take his hound back. Huge, smelly beast sheds all over everything." She sniffed. "And every time I travel anywhere, I have to find somebody...."

Allison and Kevin exchanged looks. She covered a giggle with a cough.

"Besides," Karen added with a sigh, "I did feel a *teensy* bit guilty, leaving him with you that whole two weeks the folks and I were abroad."

Allison bit her lip. Kevin frowned as if having difficulty controlling his facial muscles.

"Mom said, put an ad in the paper and find him a home." Karen folded her arms decisively. "But I think I'll just drop him off at a shelter, let them deal with him."

"I'll take Bear," Allison heard herself say. "I don't know how I'll keep him home – can't tie him forever, but…."

Kevin looked at her a long moment, then shrugged. "Bear's a smart, determined dog, but I bet we can figure some way to keep him in. What if we dig a trench, fill it with concrete and re-set the fence? If that doesn't work…."

Allison stopped him with a kiss. She liked the sound of *we*.

Bear's tail flicked back and forth over the lawn.

~

A Girl Knows

by Audrey Eggers

Girl, the neighbor's collie, met me at the car as I pulled into my driveway. She yapped. She stepped nervously. She drilled me with her big brown eyes. With her entire being she insisted that I investigate. As if she knew that was my job.

I'm Sandy Tonkins, the first female police chief of a small town in southwest Oklahoma.

"OK, Girl. I get it. Where are we going?"

She led me to Elaine's pool next door and to Elaine floating, face down, near the skimmer. I lifted a badly scratched arm and checked for pulse, but had no doubt Elaine was dead.

Girl yapped again and led me first to bloody marks on the side of the pool, then to two chaise lounges with damp towels and drinks, no ice, warm to the touch. Then Girl led me to a pair of men's prescription sunglasses. She sat and looked at me expectantly.

I reached into my pocket for the ever-present evidence bag. "Looks like you've solved it. Unless I miss my guess these will turn out to be Travis Richard's."

Girl snarled, growled and snapped her teeth.

"Way to go. Good Girl. You left us some bite marks for evidence?"

Girl barked her agreement and lay down, head resting on outstretched paws. Case closed. Now there was time to grieve.

~

Judith Sexton is a farmer's daughter, sailor's wife, former nurse, secretary, respiratory therapist, social worker, vacuum cleaner sales woman and catfish farmer. Her writing involves the senses and will keep you reading for the pure pleasure. But that ladylike prose can lead you right into a brick wall. This southern belle hails from Oklahoma's own "Little Dixie."

~

Still Life With Lemons

by Judith Sexton

The last time Mom called Aunt Eleanor, Preston answered the phone and said that Eleanor had suffered a stroke and was unable to talk. He hung up before she could ask any questions. Mom was worried, but she had a deadline at work and couldn't fly out to Los Angeles just then. I was going to spend spring break with my boyfriend at Berkeley, and she asked me to go see the old lady.

Aunt Eleanor, my grandmother's sister, was little more to me than a photograph of an elegant woman with a chignon of dark and silver hair and a wine velvet dress, and memories from a family vacation when I was about eight years old. I recalled a warm laughing voice, and when I smelled gardenias I always thought of her perfume. She was an art historian and lived for years in Europe, married late and had no children. Her husband Preston was a retired military officer. I had never met him, but Mom didn't like him. She said he was a rigid, irritable man who always looked as if he needed a laxative and she never understood why Aunt Eleanor married him. And she was concerned that Eleanor was so far away from her family, with only Preston to care for her.

I called Aunt Eleanor's house soon after we got to Jeff's apartment from the airport. Her husband answered. He sounded annoyed at first, but when he understood who I was he became friendlier.

"Allison! Of course. You're Patricia's daughter. Eleanor has always been so fond of your mother," he said. "The poor dear can't speak because of the stroke. Her mind is not affected, but she's not responding to treatment as well as one would hope."

When I asked if she could have visitors, he was quick to invite me to lunch the following day. He asked me to be there at eleven forty-five, and to please call him Uncle Preston. I hung up thinking that perhaps "Uncle Preston" wasn't so bad after all.

I looked forward to seeing the house again. My childhood memories were of huge rooms filled with light and music, window seats to curl up in, deep soft sofas, and bowls of cut flowers. And a yard with wonderful flowers and real lemons and oranges growing on trees.

Jeff wasn't familiar with the area, and I was a couple of minutes late when he dropped me off. The house was one of those big old Southern California Spanish places, mellow gold stucco with a red tile roof. Huge clay pots filled with ivy geranium stood on either side of the wide doors. When I rang the bell, a musical chime sounded. As I waited to be let in, I breathed deeply of the fragrant air. It smelled heavenly, of warm dry earth, orange and lemon blossoms and a hint of the ocean.

When Preston opened the door, he glanced at his watch before greeting me and introducing himself. He wore a faint look of annoyance, and I began by apologizing.

"No, no, my dear. It's just that the nurse has already left for the day. You're fine. And such a pretty girl! My poor sweetheart is so excited about your visit."

He was a shortish lean man, not bad looking for an old guy, but not attractive either. His forehead was creased with deep lines, and the frown crevices which bracketed a tight thin-lipped mouth made him look crabby. He led the way down the hall like a general on the march.

The house was dim after the bright sunlight, and its thick walls shut out the noise of the city. A bird sang somewhere in the house, and the only other sound was the faint hum of air conditioning. The air was stale and I wondered why the windows weren't open on such a beautiful day.

Aunt Eleanor was in a wheel chair in the den. I didn't recognize her. Her hair was short, tinted and pouffed so that she looked like any other old lady. One side of her mouth drooped, but she wore candy-pink lipstick, almost the same shade as her frilly blouse. The lipstick was glommed on thick and extended beyond the lines of her lips, giving her a pathetic clown's smile. I could smell her too-sweet tea rose perfume from across the room.

"Aunt Eleanor?" Her dark eyes met mine, her gaze intent and unblinking.

Remembering that she couldn't speak, I knelt beside her and reached for her hand. It was cold and stiff, and I realized that she couldn't even move her arms.

Uncle Preston dropped a kiss on her cheek and left us alone. I was so shocked by the changes in my aunt that I couldn't think of anything to say. I tried to be cheerful. I talked about my mom and her sisters, my sister and our cousins, bringing her up to date on all the family happenings.

She stared at my face as I talked. I had the feeling that she was pleading, that something she wanted desperately to say was locked inside her head but I had no idea how to help her. *Surely*, I thought, *there must be some way for her to communicate. Maybe by blinking, or with one of those special computers*. I was surprised that Preston hadn't already figured out something.

Unable to think of anything else to talk about, I looked around the room. New-looking furniture in tweedy browns lined up along the walls on a pale brown carpet. A large modern painting, all lines and angles provided the only color. And a few magazines which were neatly arranged on a low table. A Bonsai, a little tortured and stunted oak tree, was positioned on a stand exactly in the middle of the only window. There were no bright soft pillows, no cuddly cashmere throws, none of the deep, rich color that I recalled from my childhood visit. Then there had been miles of dark polished wood floors, and magical carpets patterned with birds and apricot trees. And I remembered a pair of huge fluffy smoke-blue cats with golden eyes who liked to sleep in the windows.

Preston came back into the room, smiling cheerfully. "Lunch is served ladies." He pushed Aunt Eleanor's chair into what he called the breakfast room. It was small and bright, with a French window which could open onto the patio. A tiny bird, a finch I think, twittered and fluttered in a cage.

Preston placed Eleanor's chair at the table, then repositioned it a bit to the left and set the brake. "Since it's only the three of us, I thought we'd eat in here, instead of the dining room. Rosalia prepared a nice roast for our lunch." He turned to me. "We always have our main meal in the middle of the day. It isn't healthy to eat a large dinner in the evening."

The food was on the table, and I saw that either Preston or the absent Rosalia had cut Aunt Eleanor's portions into small pieces on her plate. Before serving himself, Preston held a tiny piece of meat to Eleanor's lips.

"Come on, sweetheart," he coaxed. "Just try this good beef. It will help you regain your strength.

"Allison, if you will, please help yourself. You are family, and we won't stand on ceremony. I always help Eleanor with her meal while I eat."

I filled my plate. Preston took a bite for himself, then held another bite for Eleanor until she took it and began to chew slowly.

Preston made conversation, the way an older person talks to a younger one they don't know. He asked where I went to school, and what was my major, and mentioned places I must see in L.A. And all the time, he was tenderly feeding Eleanor.

Eleanor drooled as she ate, and I was uncomfortable watching, but I didn't want to *not* look at her because I didn't want her to feel left out. I watched the small bird cling on the side of its cage peering out at the wild birds in the lemon tree just beyond the patio. I wondered where Jeff was and wished I was with him. Lunch lasted forever.

Preston was a fussy little man, but I was impressed and relieved by his patience with his wife. He gently though insistently gave Aunt Eleanor her food until she had eaten all the meat and almost everything else on her plate. After each bite he dabbed her mouth and chin with the linen napkin. When he decided she had eaten enough, he pushed her chair away from the table and excused himself for a moment.

After he left the room, Eleanor's dark eyes met mine once more with that wordless plea. Then Preston returned with a lipstick, and re-colored her lips cotton candy pink. It was a small thing to do, and the lipstick looked awful, but I thought it was so sweet of him to try to make her look pretty.

"Allison, your visit has been delightful. I'm sorry we have to cut our time short, but it's time for Eleanor's nap now. You must come back to see us."

I said polite goodbyes, relieved that it was time for me to go, and leaned over to kiss Aunt Eleanor. Tears welled in her eyes, and spilled silently down her cheeks.

"Now, now, sweetheart. I've let you get too tired." Preston blotted her tears with a pink tissue. "You'll feel better when you've rested." He ushered me out with hardly another word.

I called Jeff with my cell phone, and waited out front until he came to pick me up. It was good to be outside of that still house, out where I could smell lemon blossoms and the distant ocean and hear the sounds of life. I almost wished I hadn't come. My beautiful memories of the house were spoiled, and I had hated seeing Aunt Eleanor so helpless. I thought I would rather be dead than so dependent.

That night when I called Mom, I told her all about my visit to Eleanor. Mom hadn't known how badly Aunt Eleanor was affected by her stroke, and she cried as we talked. Wanting to make her feel better, I told her how gentle Preston was with Eleanor.

"He's really kind to her," I said. "He calls her his sweetheart. And he is so patient with her. He gave her little tiny bites of food, and it took him almost an hour just to feed her some roast beef. And after she finished eating, he even put lipstick on her. He was just so sweet."

My mother caught her breath. When she spoke, her voice was tight and choked. "Eleanor has been a vegetarian all her life," she said, "and she never wears lipstick."

~

Audrey Eggers attended and graduated from Oklahoma State University, became engaged on the fourth floor of the Student Union, served as campus ministry director and international student ministry coordinator for her church, and pushed her first grandson in the swings of the University Apartment playgrounds. The campus is as familiar as her own back yard, and the students, faculty and staff are among her closest friends. So it feels completely natural to set her fiction in and around OSU and blend the university calendar into a plot.

~

Tagged

by Audrey Eggers

"You said you and your fiancé were both enrolled at the university. This house is only three blocks from campus."

Eager to see the inside of what might turn out to be hers and Darren's first home, Leanne Rogers came around the corner of the house. But Sylvia Rafferty grabbed her elbow and turned her a quarter turn. "It's a lovely neighborhood. Mrs. Weber lives next door," Ms. Rafferty said, gesturing to the south. "She's a widow and very romantic. When she finds out you're newlyweds, she'll probably spoil you rotten."

Leanne blushed. "We'd like our privacy."

"Oh, she won't intrude. But she will bring you fresh baked cinnamon rolls, pies and cakes. She'll offer to water your plants while you're away and feed your pets. Honestly, you'll love her."

“She's waving. Should we go over to meet her?”

“Oh, no. You’ll have plenty of time to meet her after you move in.”

Leanne wondered why Sylvia didn't want to talk to the neighbor if she was so loveable.

Insisting that Leanne give attention to each feature, Sylvia prattled on about the nicely paved street, the shade trees, and the quaint look of the shutters as she led Leanne up the porch steps. She unlocked the door and held it open, welcoming Leanne inside.

“The carpet’s new, and every room’s freshly painted. We chose neutral colors so the new tenants could decorate however they liked. If you want another color....”

“I prefer a neutral background. Is there some reason there’s new carpet?”

Sylvia’s face froze. “What do you mean?”

This lady is strange, Leanne thought. Aloud, she said, “I was just wondering if there was a problem with having pets in the house. I thought maybe the previous renter had pets that ruined the carpets.”

“No, no. Of course, it's all right for you to have pets.”

The room they had entered was a comfortably large living room with windows in two walls. In the center of another wall were two recessed shelves in the shape of a square with an arched top. Leanne immediately pictured her collection of bottles and water globes arranged there. An arched opening in the fourth wall led to a hallway with a cozy kitchen on one end and two bedrooms on the other.

“There are telephone jacks in both bedrooms, the living room and the hall. But the wires all had to run outside the walls. I think they did a good job.” Sylvia pointed out the wires that ran discreetly along baseboards and doorframes.

Most of the wires were camouflaged by paint, but a new unpainted telephone junction box caught Leanne’s eye. It sat crookedly on the baseboard, and a new wire ran from it up to a jack in another recessed shelf in the hallway.

"You'll want to look at the closets."

Leanne tuned out Sylvia's chatter as she dreamed of decorating the rooms. The bedroom furniture her grandparents had given her would go in the east bedroom. The highboy would exactly fit that space between the window and the corner of the room. They would use the sheets they'd received as a shower gift and the burgundy and green comforter her aunt had given them. The other bedroom would accommodate the desk, computer, shelves and the loveseat that made into a single bed. They'd drape her grandmother's afghan on the loveseat and add one or two throw pillows.

Sylvia grasped her elbow and tugged her back into the hall. "The floor furnace doesn't work. You'll probably want to cover it with a rug. The house is heated by this wall furnace." She patted the front of the heater as she walked into the kitchen.

Assuring herself that she could put up with Sylvia's pushing, steering and directing long enough to see the house, Leanne opened the door next to the furnace. She was disappointed to see the bathroom sink hung at a slant from the wall with pipes exposed beneath. Cracked linoleum rolled up in the corners of the room and next to the tub. A bare bulb hung from the center of the ceiling. An extension cord reached from there to a cup hook on the wall above the mirror, looped, knotted and dangled from a skinny, rusting towel bar. The walls were dingy, stained and peeling.

"Don't you want to see the kitchen?"

"This bathroom is so ugly."

"Oh, you'll get loads of pretty towels as wedding gifts. With new shower curtains, bath rugs and towels, this room will brighten right up. You'll be surprised."

She tugged on Leanne's elbow again. "The kitchen is

equipped with a stove and refrigerator. You know not all rentals are. What colors did you plan for your kitchen?"

Leanne looked over her shoulder at the depressing bathroom, but decided to go along with Sylvia for now and look at the kitchen. Sylvia probably never heated anything in her own kitchen other than take out, but she was busily pretending that every bride was a reincarnation of Donna Reed or the Beaver's mom.

Sylvia's high heels clicked across the floor. "We can leave this way. I'm sure you'd like to see the little back yard. There's even a doghouse. Do you have a dog?" Leading the way through the back door, Sylvia chatted about the low rent for such a prime location near campus and urged Leanne to make a quick decision before some other lucky young couple snapped it up.

"Oh, damn," she said under her breath when she reached for the gate. A padlock and chain held the gate securely closed.

Leanne thought Sylvia was much more upset than the locked gate warranted. "I'd like one last look through the house anyway." As she went back into the house, she heard Sylvia sputtering mild curses. She even kicked the gatepost.

Ignoring the bathroom, Leanne wandered through the rooms and imagined their borrowed furniture, wedding gifts and love turning the cozy little house into their first home together. She hugged her arms and twirled to face Sylvia who had finally followed her into the house. "We'll take it."

Sylvia's face, which had been pinched into a scowl since she'd tried to open the gate, relaxed into a smile. "Wonderful. I'm sure you'll be very happy here."

As they walked out the front door, Sylvia swept her arm in a dramatic gesture toward the campus. "You'll love this street in the spring. The redbud trees, the lilacs, the tulips and jonquils. It's simply beautiful."

A flutter of yellow caught Leanne's eye. She turned around to see a yellow strip of plastic tied to the porch railing. POLICE LINE – DO NOT CROSS was printed along its length. Grasping the tape near the knot, she slowly ran it through her fingers. She looked at Sylvia for an explanation.

"That was just a...an incident with the last tenant. Nothing to worry about."

Sylvia was obviously worried about something. She had worked hard enough to keep Leanne from noticing the police tape. Leanne recalled a murder the previous spring. The body had been found in a house close to campus.

"That girl that was murdered. Was that here?"

"It's nothing to be concerned about."

"They never found out who did it. Did they?"

"Look. We'll knock another twenty-five off the rent."

"I'll have to talk to Darren."

"OK. We'll knock fifty off the rent. You'll save $600 on a year's lease. Your young man told you to choose anything that you wanted."

"This is different."

"Oh, all right." The scowl returning to her face, Sylvia moved to untie the offending tape. "Call me when you decide."

"May I keep that?"

Sylvia looked at the tape and shrugged. "Sure. Why not? I certainly don't have any use for it."

Darren said, "If you like the house, it's OK with me. It will be good to save the $600." But her parents urged her to at least contact her dad's friend on the police force before making a final decision.

Captain Raymond Snyder told her the neighborhood had always been a safe one except for that murder. "She either left her door unlocked or knew her killer and let him in herself. There was no sign of forced entry."

"Do you know it was a man?"

"She was raped before she was murdered. With the rape and the fight she put up when he beat her, we have enough physical evidence to convict if we can just find a suspect. And he has to know that. He'll stay away from that house."

"There's a new phone jack in the hall and new wiring. I assume that means the phone was jerked loose?"

"You make a pretty good detective."

"This probably sounds presumptuous, but did you check the redial button?"

"It only dialed the nine. She tried to call for help."

He told her that the local paper had done a good job of covering the story. She could read the old issues and learn all the information the police and DA were willing to make public. He even offered to call her parents and assure them of her safety.

Leanne went to the newspaper office and asked to see all the articles they had published about the murder. The paper described the crime as a brutal rape and murder. The first article said that Cindy Trent's body had been found in the living room, but there was blood on the floors, walls and furniture of almost every room. Leanne suspected they meant all but the bathroom. The murderer had apparently searched for something, but money, a computer and a portable CD player had all been left behind.

The paper speculated that this rape tied in with the series of rapes that had spread over several months, but Leanne remembered that a man had been arrested and convicted of those crimes.

Neighbors and friends had been interviewed by reporters. One neighbor was nearly deaf and turned her hearing aid off at night in order to sleep. That would be Mrs. Weber. Cindy was murdered sometime during the first weekend of spring break. The other friends and neighbors were out of town at the time.

They described Cindy as intelligent with "an almost photographic memory for names and phone numbers." They said she was always cautious and reminded her friends to lock their doors.

As Leanne gathered the pen and papers she had used to take notes, a young woman approached her. "Hi. I'm Judy Abrahms. Sam said someone had come in to get information about Cindy Trent's murder. I thought the family might have hired a private investigator. But you look a little young for that."

"It's more of a personal interest. I'm thinking of moving into her house."

"Wow!"

"It's been cleaned up. Repainted, carpeted."

"Yeah, I knew the police had turned it back over to the owner. I guess he's pretty anxious to start getting some income from it."

Remembering Sylvia Rafferty, Leanne said, "If his rental agent is any indication, I'd say you're right."

"I'd think you'd want to put all this out of your mind--if you're going to live there."

"Well, I started out just trying to find out if I thought it was safe. But now. I don't know. I really care. I want him caught. I want him to pay for what he did to her."

"Let me tell you some of what I know that didn't come out in the paper. Cindy Trent wasn't what you'd call pretty, but she had this real..." Judy paused searching for the right word. "...real vibrant personality. Her friends were crazy about her."

Leanne watched Judy's eyes as she talked. Judy had obviously been deeply affected by what she had learned about Cindy Trent.

"She took care of people. You read in one of the articles

that she warned her friends to lock their doors. She took them soup if they had a cold. She practically adopted the woman next door as her grandmother."

"I've seen Mrs. Weber, but I haven't met her yet."

"You will. The other thing that might be helpful is the reason Cindy Trent was in town that weekend."

"It was the start of spring break, right?"

"Right. She had a dog, a puppy really, at the vet school hospital. She couldn't pick him up until Monday."

As Leanne left she thanked Judy for all the information. "I think I'll go to the rental agency and borrow the key to look at the house again before making a final decision."

Judy said, "I'm what passes for the crime reporter here. But in a town this size, that usually means I'm writing little blurbs about plants stolen off front porches. What you said before about caring?" Leanne nodded. "This case really got to me."

Leanne sank to the floor and rubbed her hand across the carpet. Were there blood stains and the remains of a chalk outline under this new carpet? Leanne was filled with a surge of compassion for the girl who had suffered and died here. Her own sister had been sexually molested when she was five years old. Leanne had listened to Marissa cry during the night for years. She had hugged Marissa tight until she fell to sleep again and had continued to share a room even though she could have had her own.

Leanne jumped up from the floor and her face took on an expression of determination. Her sister's abuser had gone to another state where the statute of limitations had run out, and he couldn't be extradited. If she could avenge this rape and murder, she could in a way avenge her own sister's suffering.

"I'll try," she vowed. "I will try."

* * *

Final arrangements for the wedding, moving Darren's and Leanne's possessions into the house, and contacting the phone company and utilities, all had to be taken care of. Leanne was busier than she ever remembered being, but she took time to talk with Mrs. Weber when brought a banana cream pie to welcome them to the neighborhood.

"Oh, thank you. This is Darren's favorite. And strawberry shortcake just barely edges it out of first place for me," Leanne told her. "Stay and have a piece with me."

They spent a while getting acquainted before Leanne brought the conversation around to Cindy Trent.

"I hope you don't think I'm just being curious."

Mrs. Weber laid her hand on Leanne's arm. "No, dear. It's nice to have someone to talk to about Cindy. I really miss her." She was silent for a moment and then said, "It may seem strange that two people so far apart in age could be good friends. But, you see, we both had such a love for animals."

"Was the dog house Cindy's?"

"Yes, Cindy brought her dog with her when she came to college. She'd had him for twelve years. And then he just got sick and died."

"Oh, no."

Mrs. Weber tightened her lips and nodded. "I brought over some of her favorite cookies and listened while Cindy told me all about him. She showed me his old collar. Then she cried while she held his shiny new tag in her hand. The day before that dog died, she'd taken him for his shots. She hadn't even had the chance to put the new tag on his collar."

"I understood she had a dog at the vet's when she died."

"Yes. I convinced Cindy to get a new puppy. And she did love him. She was so worried that week when the puppy got sick. I thought she was going to take him home to the vet there, but Cindy took her puppy over to the hospital, the one at the vet school."

"So you thought she had already gone home."

Mrs. Weber nodded and pulled out a tissue to wipe her eyes and nose. "I found out later. She planned to pick the dog up Monday morning and drive home. Her parents called the police when she didn't arrive."

Leanne wondered if anyone realized how much Mrs. Weber grieved over Cindy Trent.

"I've kept you too long, dear," Mrs. Weber said. "I'll run along and let you get on with your work. We'll have plenty of time to talk while you're living here."

Leanne followed her to the door. "Did you tell the police all this?"

"Well, not about the dog that died. I didn't think it mattered."

"It probably doesn't. But you never can tell what information will help the police put the whole story together."

"You're right, dear. I'll give them a call."

Leanne stood on the porch and waved as Mrs. Weber walked back to her house. Leanne called out, "Come back to see me again."

Mrs. Weber turned and smiled. "Thanks. I'll do that."

Leanne dropped a box onto the love seat and grabbed the ringing phone in the hall. "You asked me to call to see if your phone was working," said her mother.

While they talked Darren came in. He planted a kiss on Leanne's open mouth and wrapped her fingers around a shiny new key. "The key to my heart," he whispered in her ear.

Leanne opened her hand to look at the key just as Darren patted her behind. She jumped and the key fell out of her hand and into the floor furnace.

"Darren! Mom, I gotta go. I just dropped my key in the furnace. I'll talk to you later. Darren! Come back in here."

"What happened?"

"The key to your heart just fell in the floor furnace. And we're getting married in five days. What are we going to do?"

"Don't worry about it. When I was a kid, we were always dropping stuff into the floor furnace. I'm pretty good at getting it out."

He went out to his car and came back with two screwdrivers, one of them big enough to adjust the forward thrust engine on the starship Enterprise. Working the big screwdriver's flat tip under the lip of the grate, he worked halfway around the furnace. "Here," he said to Leanne. "You take the other one and keep the opposite side from slipping back."

They worked that way three times around the grate before they were able to lift it off and set it aside. So much dirt and fuzz had accumulated in the bottom of the unused furnace that the key had just sunk in.

"I was standing here, with my hand like this. It must be in that area." Leanne pointed, and Darren pushed fuzz aside to look for the key. She rummaged through boxes for a flashlight and aimed its beam into the dark hole.

"You know. It wasn't really the key to my heart," he said. "It was a new key I made for the back door. We could just go make another one."

"Wait." Leanne grabbed his arm. "Don't touch anything." She jumped up, ran to the kitchen, then darted into the bathroom and back to Darren's side.

Leanne slapped tweezers into Darren's hand. "Pick it up with these."

"Pick what up?"

"I don't know what it is. That." She pointed.

The flashlight reflected off a piece of shiny metal. Darren stretched his arm into the furnace and retrieved a round disc. "What is it?"

"A dog tag," Leanne said. She held the plastic bag for Darren to drop the tag in. "We have to be careful. This could be evidence."

When they called, Captain Snyder agreed to pick up the dog tag and promised to talk with Mrs. Weber again. Darren and Leanne went back to the busy schedule of blood tests, marriage license, prenuptial counseling, out-of-town visitors, rehearsal, and the big day itself.

A week after the wedding Leanne received a call from Sylvia Rafferty. "A potential buyer for your house is going to stop by to see it. Is it clean?"

Since no one had mentioned the house was to be shown Leanne thought the rental agent was presumptuous but true to character. "It looks OK considering we're in the process of settling in. But you can't expect us to move out so soon. We have a lease."

"Oh, don't worry. This buyer is interested in acquiring rental property. Nothing will change as far as you're concerned."

"What's the name?"

"It's Lon or something like that. If he's interested I'll get the personal information later. Just be gracious and I'll think about reimbursing you with a rent discount." A blip on the line indicated another call. "Gotta run" sufficed for Sylvia's goodbye.

Leanne had time to throw shoes into the closet, prop Darren's baseball bat in the corner and sweep Cheez-It crumbs off a table into her hand before the doorbell rang.

A man leaned against the railing with both hands in his pockets. "I assume Ms. Rafferty informed you I was coming by?"

"She just called. I'm Leanne Rogers, uh, Jansen."

"Lyndon Belden." He ignored her outstretched hand and walked past her into the living room. His eyes scanned the walls and floor. Something about his close scrutiny of the doorframe sent a frisson of caution up Leanne's spine and reminded her that Sylvia Rafferty didn't even have this guy's name. She stood by the open front door rather than following him through the house.

Belden returned to the front room and seemed more at ease. "I hear you're a newly wed." His eyes raked her figure. "I don't suppose you waited for the wedding. Most don't these days."

She heard a familiar sound, Darren's key in the back door. *Oh, please*, she prayed. *Don't let him hurt Darren.* Attempting to deflect Belden's attention, Leanne gestured toward the door and managed to send a vase crashing to the floor. "I'd like you to leave."

"Oh, I have a few things I still need to check." He leered and watched her face for a reaction. "How's your plumbing?"

"Leave now, or I'll call Captain Snyder."

He moved quickly and grabbed her wrist. "It won't be the first time someone came on to me and then threatened to call the police. Don't you want to know what it's like when the man has experience and patience?"

Darren appeared in the hallway and put a finger to his lips. He was angry but controlled. Praying that Darren had a plan, Leanne tried not to give him away by even a glance.

"You must mean Cindy."

"That little tart. First she manages to bump into me, palms my dog's tag for an excuse to call me. Then she tracks down my phone number. She invited me over here!"

"So you met her at the Vet Hospital?"

He grinned proudly. "Oh, yeah. I noticed her listening in on my conversation with the receptionist. She wanted me from the first time she laid eyes on me."

Darren, now! I can't keep this up. Why are you waiting?

"You were searching for that dog tag. The police have it now. I gave it to them."

"You're lying, little girl. I found it by the phone." He tugged at her arm, and she used his momentum to duck past him and roll away. Darren caught him across the chest with the baseball bat.

As Belden lay gasping for a breath, Captain Snyder stepped through the front door and cuffed him.

Trembling, Leanne moved into Darren's arms. "I didn't know you were going for the bat. It took so long." She turned to Captain Snyder. "But you have a gun. What were you waiting for?"

"I just arrived in time to hear you say you gave us the tag, which I was actually here to pick up. You two overpowered him before I had a chance to assess risk and come to the rescue."

He handed Leanne a short roll of police tape. "Would you mind tying that across the front porch there?"

~

Sharon K. Hudgins is an industrious seller of real estate in Cushing, Oklahoma. She has served as editor for the realtor's newsletter *CBR Banner* and the *Young at Heart* supplement of the *Cushing Daily Citizen* newspaper. She is one of six authors, jointly named Norman Moore, who wrote *The Yankee Dollar Conspiracy.* Writing friends enjoy her energy, sales acumen and varied talents when she turns all that energy and talent to the craft we love – writing.

~

Mambo

by Sharon K. Hudgins

Moss covered cypress trees hung like headless scarecrows in the full moon's light. Nearby splashes pursued us. A low bear-like growl broke the stillness as we slipped along the bayou in the flat bottom boat.

Luke answered my thought.

"Gator," he said in a whisper.

"Gator." My eyes wide and searching.

"Shhhh. They'll go away."

Captain Luke Matthews knew the bayous better than the muskrats themselves did.

"How much further to this clandestine location?" I asked.

"Listen, you can hear them now."

I listened. I heard the beat of drums and singing voices.

Luke steered the tender away from the main channel.

Only inches of stale water lapped below us, as he stepped overboard. The slimy mud oozed up his waders. Suction from the mud integrated with the sound of the night creatures.

"Sam, stay put, " he instructed.

My thoughts drifted to Angelene lying in the hospital bed. Her doe eyes, glazed and darting. Her hair, wild and frizzed. Her mulatto skin was smeared with dirt, paint and trails of tears. My fear was her daughter Makala had fallen victim to the recent rash of child disappearances.

Angelene had scuffled with a police officer. Restraints shackled her limbs. The police didn't give much to go on and Angel made little sense. She was lucky that the tall, square-jawed, Officer Daniel Carloni was on duty that night and brought her to Orleans General.

I met Daniel five years ago. It was our first night on duty. He on the police force and myself, a nurse at the hospital. Daniel had found a young boy wandering the streets. He thought the child was on drugs, but drugs were not found in his system. The nine-year old was in a trance. I briefed Daniel on the religion of voodoo and sent him to Angel's Book Boutique.

"Makala, Makala, missing. Magic Man took her. Find Makala," Angelene pleaded.

I had watched my best friend's child grow into a beautiful teen. I promised I would find Makala.

After a short time, the bushman returned, and we camouflaged the small craft and ourselves. Luke smeared muck over his face, throat and hands. He insisted I do the same. Reluctantly, I smudged on the foul-smelling grime.

"Stay close to me, Sam, and watch where you step, girlie."

I couldn't help but snicker at Luke's comment. But all the while, my heart pounded. We crept toward the chanting. Darkness from the dense forest surrounded us. My arm stretched touching Luke's back.

"How can you see where you're going?" I asked bumping into him.

"Don't move."

A hissing sound chilled my body. I froze, knowing that any moment I could be dinner. I heard Luke rustle in the shoulder bag he carried.

What is he doing? A gun? A knife? My mind bounced with thoughts. Then the moonlight glistened, through a break in the tree line, onto the scales of a fish as he tossed it into the night. I watched the phosphorescent streak and knew that the single chomp was that of a gator. In the next second, Luke grabbed my hand and rushed me blindly to safety.

"I follow my nose. Smell the gumbo," he finally said as we had slowed to a walk.

Maybe it was the power of suggestion, but the aroma of the thick okra stew was in the air. "What's the botanical scent?" I asked.

"Could be musk incense or a brew of roots and herbs... or both. Hard to know for sure."

We neared the clearing; light flickered through the bushes. I caught another glimpse of Luke's leather necklace. "What's the wooden pendant around your neck, Luke? Your Loa protector?"

"Might not be a bad idea. I've seen a lot of strange things in these here parts."

Before I had a chance to question him more, he shushed me to silence. The music had stopped. He motioned downward with his hand. We crouched in our tracks. A man's voice rumbled. "What's he saying?" I whispered.

"Gullah."

"I know he's speaking Gullah dialect, but can you understand him?"

"Something about preparing the *mambo*. This new

priestess has the blood of Makandal in her. The same blood that Marie LaVeau had in her. The present houngan is old and this one is young. They must make the young one ready and pray to the Loas."

A chill slithered up my spine at the thought of anyone actually praying to snakes.

"Marie LaVeau was the Voodoo Queen of New Orleans, but who is Makandal?"

"Makandal was a voodoo priest; a houngan from Santo Domingo. It's said he was Marie LaVeau's granddaddy."

The drums started. We began moving again toward the pulsation. Tambourines joined in, maracas, flutes and an occasional cowbell. The chanting seemed to pull us closer. The bon fire and torches guided our way.

A dance was in progress. The women undulating in one line and the men gesticulating in the other. Crayon colors of cotton skirts swayed. The men flailing their arms and whisky bottles to the rhythm.

"They dance the calinda," Luke said.

In the crowd was the Magic Man. Some believed he was clairvoyant. He danced and performed his hoodoo, magic without the religion of voodoo. He held a jug of rum in one hand and a fireball in the other. He towered over seven feet tall in his black tuxedo and tails. He also sported a black and white striped top hat similar to the *Cat in the Hat*. Children loved to watch him.

Makala had watched, but only through the French doors of her mother's shop. With the child disappearances, Angelene trusted only two people and certainly not the man in the hat.

Suddenly the Magic Man threw the fireball onto the ground. A loud shot rang out startling the spectators. An enormous, dense cloud of smoke filled the air.

"Aahhh," I gasped in unison with the onlookers as the smoke began to clear. High on the mound appeared a crucified angel. The congregation bowed in reverence.

I crawled to another bush for a better view. Something rancid was nearby. Flies swarmed the stink. A decapitated, decaying chicken hung overhead. Luke whistled his whip-poor-will warning. I obediently retreated.

Minutes seemed like hours as I watched the angel's scaly sash slink to her feet, then coil itself upward around her body. The angelic figure raised her head and stared from the devil's eyes. "Noooooo…." I moaned deep from within. It was Makala.

The Magic Man sparked another smoke bomb. He commanded the followers to silence as he spoke in tongue. He tipped his hat to the raven haired child entranced on the cross. The serpent had vanished.

Luke and I backtracked a short distance. He boosted me up a tree and ordered me to "stay put."

I strained to hear; nothing but a zombie-like hush came over the crowd. But there was another gathering below me.

Twigs faintly snapping, leaves rustling – Carloni's men had arrived. The chanting started and the men crept nearer. In the distance, a baby cried.

Anxious to join the force, I quietly searched for the walkie-talkie in my backpack. In my precarious perch atop the tree, I fumbled the unit. It landed with a thud and a growl. The ursine growl. Gators! Not Carloni's men. Gators. I was surrounded by gators.

"Luke, my men are in position," Carloni whispered over the walkie-talkie.

"I know, just a few more minutes and they'll be heading your way." Luke answered.

"Samantha O.K.?"

"She's fine, got to go, OUT."

"Fine," I muttered. "I'm not fine, I'm stuck in this tree, the radio is on the ground, my best friend is in the hospital, her daughter has been kidnapped, alligators are everywhere, it's dark and ohhh…ohhh…. A big black bird just damned near knocked me off my perch. Oh yeah, I'm fine. Oh, isn't this cozy, he wants to share my tree. No, not my limb. Shoo. This is great, I'm talking to a loon – first myself, now a loon."

Frustrated and certainly in no fear that gators could climb, I sat, waited, watched and listened. The alligators passed and another whimper from a baby. "It could be a wild cat, they sound like a baby crying or, it could be . . ."

Screams sirened from the sorcery. My binoculars focused in on a beefy woman – stampeding through the menagerie. The men – oblivious and too inebriated to realize they were surrounded by gators!

Pandemonium rushed through the cult, and they fled to their only land outlet. I could see Carloni's men as I watched the chaos at the citadel. The Magic Man threw a fireball between him and Carloni. The fire blazed a couple of afros while the smoke camouflaged the Magic Man. The smoke cleared. Carloni's gun fired. And at the end of the dart lay a motionless, but smiling, drugged alligator. The granddaddy of all alligators, and hanging out both sides of its mouth was the Magic Man's top hat.

"Sam, get down here now," Luke commanded.

I slid down the trunk with my medical bag. Luke was carrying Makala. She had been drugged, but otherwise on the initial physical examination, she was fine.

"Carloni's evidence on the child slavery ring will put them away for a long time. Come on, Sam, we got to hurry. The gators will be back soon."

"How do you know?"

Luke held the pendant from his neck and pressed his mouth to the opening and blew.

"The baby I heard crying."

"Yeah," said Luke, "and the gators think it's one of theirs, and they, so to speak, come to the rescue."

~

Sara Sue Hoklotubbe won second place for Mystery, Suspense Novel in the Johnson County Creative Writers Contest (2002) and numerous other awards for her work in fiction, nonfiction and poetry. Her first book about a young contemporary Cherokee woman, published by The University of Arizona Press, is expected to be released in 2003. Sara writes with true storyteller style, and readers enjoy the telling as well as the resolution. When she moved to Alaska from Oklahoma her critique group demanded further installments of her work. A Cherokee citizen, Sara has now returned to Oklahoma and lives near Tahlequah.

~

The Winner and The Loser

by Sara Sue Hoklotubbe

"Look at this, Gladys, we've got a local celebrity in Sycamore Springs."

Sergeant Charlie McCord released one side of the newspaper just long enough to spoon another chunk of ice into his coffee. He took a sip to see if the steamy liquid had yet reached a tolerable temperature and then returned his attention to the paper. "Says right here, 'Sycamore's Sherry Fulton Wins Lotto.' You suppose that's the same Fulton that lives over on Archer Street?" he asked.

The red-headed waitress stopped long enough to lean over the counter and read the headline for herself before continuing down the aisle and dumping a stack of dirty dishes onto a cart. "My, my, my," she said as she returned to the lunch counter. "It was bound to happen, since they started selling lottery tickets last month at the gas station over by that little honky-tonk on the Missouri state line. It doesn't take more than thirty minutes to get over there. Everybody in town has started buying gas and lottery tickets over there, including me. How much did she win?"

"One point two million," said Charlie as he raised his eyebrows. "Can you imagine that?"

"Not in my wildest dreams, honey. Looks like the economy in this little cow-poke town is about to take a turn for the better. Maybe she'll leave me a big tip next time she brings in her kids for hamburgers." Gladys placed two menus under her arm, picked up two glasses of ice water and sashayed down the aisle as a young couple entered and took a seat in a booth near the front door.

The Sergeant's radio began to spit and gurgle. He turned up the volume for a moment, took a final swig of coffee and headed for the door. "Got to go, Gladys. Duty calls."

* * *

When Charlie nosed his police car into the driveway at 2406 Cato Lane, he could see Lance Smith, one of two junior officers already on the scene. Lance met Charlie in front of the house and started reporting what he knew so far.

"It looks like she just quit breathing," said Lance. "But, I found this under the kitchen table." Lance held up a plastic bag containing a syringe. "She doesn't look like a doper, but I'm going to guess she's an overdose victim. Only problem is we didn't find drugs of any kind in the house."

"Do we know who she is?"

"Name's Cathy Westerman. According to the driver's license in her purse, she would have been twenty-eight years old next month. Looks about right."

"Anything out of place?"

"Doesn't look like it."

"What about witnesses? Friends or family around?"

"According to the neighbor lady, Mrs. Simmons, she lived by herself, was a real nice woman. Said she got worried when the dog started howling like it was hurt or something and wouldn't stop. The old lady couldn't get an answer at the front door, so she called it in. When we got here, the front door was unlocked. But, we had to call animal control before we could go in. The dog seemed to be protecting her."

Charlie looked around the front yard. An older woman stood at the edge of an adjoining driveway wringing her hands.

"Is that Mrs. Simmons?" asked Charlie.

"Yes, sir," said Lance. "We haven't told her anything yet. Figured we'd save that for you." Then he added, "The medical examiner is on the way. Should be here any time. I'm on my way to check out the garage."

"Carry on," said Charlie. Then, he entered the house to survey the scene before anyone else got a chance to stir it up. The victim lay face down on the floor where the living room, dining room and kitchen all converged into one large area. It looked like she had just finished eating lunch. The table was clean but he could still feel hot air escaping from the dishwasher. The rest of the house was tidy; everything seemed to be in order.

A laptop computer sat on the open portion of a roll-top desk. Colorful fish wiggled slowly as they swam across the screen. Charlie took a pen out of his shirt pocket and used the tip to touch the space bar on the keyboard. The fish instantly disappeared, revealing a blank email message.

He then used the pen to pull open the top desk drawer. Small compartments held an array of office supplies. Pens, pencils, paper clips and note pads all had their own space. Charlie had never seen a desk so organized.

He returned his attention to the top of the desk. In a dark corner, under the edge of the roll top portion, a spindle held several pieces of pink paper. When he looked closer, he realized they were lottery tickets. He laughed to himself when he thought about the craze that had hit the small town recently and figured it would only get worse now that they had a local millionaire, compliments of the state of Missouri.

Charlie heard a car door slam and looked up to see Doc Sanger, the local physician who also served as the county coroner, walking toward the house. The fish resumed their swimming and Charlie walked to the door and opened it for the doctor. The two men shook hands and exchanged pleasantries. Then the doctor retrieved two latex gloves from his pocket and pulled them onto his outstretched hands one at a time.

"What do we have hear, Charlie?" asked the doctor.

Charlie placed both hands on his knees as he bent down to watch the doctor examine the victim. "I like to leave the diagnosis stuff up to you professionals," said Charlie.

"Well, she's definitely dead," said the doctor.

"About how long you think?"

"Not very," he said. "I'd guess she expired in the last couple of hours. I'll be able to give you more information after we get her in and I can examine the body more closely."

Charlie stood up just as Lance stepped back into the kitchen from an outside door that led to the garage. Two young men in paramedic uniforms arrived and with the doctor barking orders at them, they covered and removed the body.

When they were gone, Charlie looked at Lance and said, "Do you know how to turn off that computer over there?"

Lance nodded.

"Check it for fingerprints, first. Then I want one of those computer hackers at the station to see if they can tell us who she was talking to on that thing. Then secure the house and get that paraphernalia to the lab so we can see what her drug of choice was. Looks pretty open and shut. Should be able to wrap it up in short order."

"Yes, sir."

When Charlie exited the front door, he could see the neighbor, Mrs. Simmons had stopped wringing her hands. She had moved to the steps of her porch.

Charlie walked over to her and waited for her to stop crying before he spoke. "Excuse me, ma'am, would you mind if I asked you a few questions?"

Mrs. Simmons removed her glasses and wiped her face with a handkerchief before looking at the Sergeant. "What happened to her?" she asked weakly.

"We're not sure yet, ma'am. How well did you know Miss Westerman?"

"She moved in about six months ago. Doesn't have any family, I don't think. She was the sweetest thing. Just lived there with her dog. Kind of reminded me of my daughter that lives in Seattle." The old lady began to sob again.

Charlie took a card out of his shirt pocket and handed it to her. "When you feel like talking, would you mind calling me at this number?"

She took his card, nodded and then asked, "What's going to happen to Clinton?"

"Clinton?" asked Charlie.

"Cathy's dog. He wouldn't hurt a flea." The woman smiled and then said, "She named him Clinton because he chased all the female dogs on the block."

Charlie grimaced in an effort to contain a laugh.

"I'd be glad to take him in," she said. "He likes me."

"I'm sure Roy down at the dog pound would be more than happy for you to take him off his hands. If he's got any doubts, have him call me. But, if she's got some kin that comes along who want him, you'll have to give him up."

"OK," Mrs. Simmons nodded.

Charlie headed back to his cruiser as Lance and another officer strung yellow crime-scene tape across the front door. As he drove toward the Dixie Diner, he continued to think about the scene he had just left. He had picked up more than his fair share of dead vagrants and drunks. He'd seen plenty of people, rich and poor, ruin their lives with drugs. In the end they all seemed to be the same. They were people who had lost the joy of living. Hopeless, with nothing to live for, they numbed their pain any way they could – even to their deaths. But, he couldn't help but think this woman was different. He had a sixth sense about these things, and right now it told him something wasn't right about this case. But, he would wait for the autopsy and start there.

* * *

Charlie didn't have to wait long. Less than twenty-four hours later, he was sitting across the table from Doc Sanger.

"She died from anaphylactic shock," said the doctor.

Charlie scratched his head. "What causes that, Doc?"

"Lots of things can cause it," he said. "It just depends on what a person is drastically allergic to, like a drug or a bee sting. It can be fatal if the victim doesn't get to a doctor or administer their own shot of epinephrine. Some people with acute allergies keep vials of epinephrine on hand for just such an occasion. It looks like she might have been trying to do that, with a puncture on her right thigh. But, she must have been too late. We'll have to wait for the lab to see if any got into her bloodstream."

Suddenly, Charlie remembered the syringe. "So, she didn't overdose on drugs?"

"Again, we'll have to wait on the lab work, but I don't think so. More than likely, something she ate. I didn't find any signs of an insect bite or sting."

"Could you tell what she had eaten?" asked Charlie.

"It appears to me the victim had eaten a salad of some sort, mostly green, and then some sort of a chocolate desert. Maybe a cookie or a brownie."

Charlie's radio crackled and he heard his call number. Lance was trying to get in touch. Charlie thanked the doctor and returned to his cruiser where he could carry on a conversation with his colleague in private on a phone.

"You aren't going to believe this, Sarge," said Lance.

"Try me."

"You know that syringe we picked up over at the Westerman place?"

"Go ahead."

"It didn't have drugs in it."

"Epinephrine?"

"Do what?"

"Did it have epinephrine in it? Kind of like adrenalin for allergic reactions."

"No, sir, nothing but H2O."

"Pardon me."

"All that syringe had in it was water."

The airwaves fell silent.

"Are you there, Sarge?"

"Yeah, I'm here. Meet me over at the Westerman place. I think this is beginning to smell."

* * *

Charlie parked behind Lance and the two police officers met on the front porch. The morning paper, rolled tightly and secured with a green rubber band, lay on the welcome mat. Lance slid the paper out of the way with the toe of his boot as Charlie broke the yellow tape and the two men entered the house.

"By the way," said Charlie, "did the so-called experts find anything unusual on the girl's computer?"

"No, sir," said Lance. "But they are still working on it."

The officers stood in the middle of the room with their hands on their hips, looking around. Finally, Lance spoke.

"What are we looking for, Sarge?"

"Something Cathy Westerman was so allergic to that it killed her," said Charlie as he opened the refrigerator.

"But, Sarge, if she was that allergic to something wouldn't she know it? I mean, I doubt she would have a refrigerator full of dairy products if she was allergic to milk."

"Yeah, I know. Just see if you can find anything that looks out of the ordinary. I'll make a note of what's in the fridge here. You check the trash."

Charlie opened the refrigerator and found it stocked with fresh and frozen vegetables, diet soda and soy milk. He could see no meat anywhere. "Must be one of those vegetarians," he muttered.

"There's nothing in the trash except yesterday's newspaper," said Lance. "No food here."

After checking the kitchen, Charlie moved over to the roll-top desk where the computer had been yesterday. He searched the other two drawers he hadn't looked in the day before. "This is the most organized woman I've ever seen," said Charlie. "She's even got her bills filed in alphabetical order."

Lance joined the Sergeant and together they sifted through Cathy Westerman's records. Finally, the Sarge picked up the spindle which held dozens of lottery tickets.

"Can you believe the money people waste on these

things?"

"You never know," laughed Lance. "There's a woman on the other side of town that doesn't think it's too big a waste."

Charlie thumbed through the lottery tickets and something caught his eye. "Look at this, Lance," he said. "Every last one of these tickets have the same numbers on them. She must have been playing the same numbers every time she played." Charlie sat the spindle back down and then picked it back up again. "Except for the one on top. It's different. Wonder why she changed?"

"Maybe she thought her luck would change with a different set of numbers."

"Maybe so." Charlie squinted his eyes and looked into space for a moment. "Lance, did you say yesterday's paper was in the trash?"

"Yeah."

"Dig it out. I want to check something."

Lance pulled the paper out of the trash and handed it to Charlie.

Charlie pulled out a chair, sat down and proceeded to spread the paper out on the kitchen table. He thumbed through several pages until he found the list of winning lottery numbers and said, "Bring me that stack of lottery tickets over here, would you, Lance?"

Lance complied and the Sergeant studied the tickets for a moment. Then Charlie leaned back in his chair and said, "This is interesting. She's got the winning number on every ticket except the one for yesterday. If she had kept buying the same numbers, she would have been the big winner instead of that Fulton lady."

"Maybe we better verify exactly who bought that winning ticket," said Lance.

"Let's go," said Charlie as they both headed out the door. "You can ride with me."

* * *

Sherry Fulton invited the two officers in. “With all the media hounding me, I’ve had to take my phone off the hook,” she said. “You wouldn’t believe all the strangers who are asking for a handout. It hasn’t sunk in how much money I’ve really won. Now, what was your question?”

“Do you know a woman named Cathy Westerman?” asked Charlie.

“Oh, the woman they found dead yesterday?” she asked. “I read about her in the paper today. No, I don’t know her. Why do you ask?”

“Can you tell us where you were around noon yesterday?”

Sherry became defensive. “Why are you asking me these insane questions?”

“If you want to make it hard, we can take you in to the station for questioning.”

“If you must know, I was at my lawyer’s office all day yesterday. Now that I don’t need his money, I’m divorcing this loser I’m married to. And I’m trying to figure out how to keep his sticky hands off my fortune.”

“Can you tell us where you bought your lottery ticket?”

“I didn’t buy it,” she replied. “It was a gift … from my husband’s aunt. And if you need any more information from me you can call my lawyer and get in line with the rest of the fruitcakes.” She turned on her heels and left the room.

Charlie and Lance let themselves out and returned to Charlie’s police car. “What now, Sarge?” asked Lance.

The static on Charlie’s car radio began to pop. Through the mixture of sounds, Charlie picked up his transmitter and answered. According to the dispatcher, Doc Sanger was looking for him. “Tell him I’m on my way to his office right now," said Charlie.

When Charlie and Lance got to the doctor's office, Doc Sanger agreed to fit them in between patients. "Just thought you'd want the rest of this lab report," said the doctor. "My best guess right now is that your victim died from peanuts."

"How do you know that?"

"Just got to thinking and called over to the pharmacy. My niece works over there. Asked her if she'd look up Cathy Westerman's prescription for epinephrin and see if it listed her allergies on it. Sure enough, the original prescription came from a doctor in Tulsa. It was written for an allergic reaction to peanuts. So, I ran a test for peanuts on the contents of her stomach, and there you are." The doctor handed Charlie a copy of a fax from a nearby lab. "Says there were traces of peanuts in whatever she ate that day."

"Traces?" asked Charlie.

"That's all it takes to kill someone if they are that allergic."

"I'll be," said Lance. "So it could have just been an accident?"

"That's your job," said the doctor. "I've got to get back to work." The doctor closed the door and called for the next patient.

* * *

Charlie and Lance got into Charlie's cruiser and contemplated the case of Cathy Westerman on their way to the new hangout for lottery aficionados over on the state line. The gas station looked bright and clean with gas pumps right out of the future. Two young men worked behind the counter, one collecting money for gas and the other selling lottery tickets. Charlie took out a ten dollar bill and the two men got in the lottery line. A few seconds later, Charlie was picking numbers to put on his lottery ticket.

Lance shoved two dollars toward the young man and said, "I'll take a quick pick."

"Big spender," teased Charlie. Then he began to collect information. "Say, young fellow, are you the one who sold the winning ticket a few days ago?"

The young man's eyes lit up. "Yes, sir."

"Well, how about that. Did you get a cut of the winnings?" inquired Charlie.

"The gas station won a percentage for selling the winning ticket and the boss gave me a $1,000 bonus." The young man beamed.

"Do you remember the person who bought it?"

"No, not really. We sell so many tickets in here, there's no way I could remember, but I'm the only one who sells tickets from eight to five everyday. So the bonus should be mine."

Charlie pointed to a video camera stationed above the door and asked, "Do you think a picture of the person would be on the tape from the camera?"

"I suppose so. We record video in case we get robbed."

"Do you think I could see that tape?" asked Charlie.

The young man picked up the phone and a few moments later the manager appeared to see what the hubbub was all about. He offered Charlie and Lance some coffee and the duo followed him to the back office where he selected a tape for the requested day. Then he handed Charlie the remote. "Here you go," he said. "You will have to pick her out of the gazillion people that bought tickets that day. Have fun." And with that he turned on his heels and left the officers alone.

After an hour of fast forward and rewind, Lance yelled, "Stop. Back up. I recognized someone."

Charlie slowly rewound the tape until he, too,

recognized a woman standing at the counter buying lottery tickets. It was Cathy Westerman's neighbor, Mrs. Simmons.

Charlie ejected the tape and explained to the manager he needed the tape for a murder investigation. He could give it to them now, or wait until Lance retrieved a warrant.

The manager gasped. "Take it. By all means take it."

* * *

When the two officers parked in front of Mrs. Simmons' house, she was sitting on the front porch next to a large German shepherd. The dog stood up and started barking as they approached the house.

Mrs. Simmons petted the dog and told him it was all right. The dog stopped barking and sat down.

"Clinton's OK," said Mrs. Simmons. "I think he's looking for Cathy all of the time. Poor dear. Come on in."

Charlie and Lance followed the woman inside where she invited them to sit at the kitchen table. The dog lay down near the back door.

"Would you like some brownies?" she asked as she slid a plate stacked high onto the center of the table. "They are my specialty – fresh out of the oven." Then she handed each man a napkin.

Immediately, Charlie noticed a large jar of peanut butter sitting on the table. He picked it up and held it in the air. "By the way Mrs. Simmons, did you know – "

Suddenly, Clinton, jumped to his feet and started barking.

"Isn't that the funniest thing?" asked Mrs. Simmons. "My nephew taught him to bark every time someone touches that jar. I don't know why he did that."

Charlie put the container back down and Mrs. Simmons opened the back door allowing the dog to exit into the backyard.

"Now, what were you saying, Sergeant?" she asked.

"Did you know Cathy Westerman was allergic to peanuts?"

"Allergic to peanuts?" she repeated.

"That's why she died," he said. "She ingested some peanuts, the allergic response cut off her ability to breathe."

"Oh, my –" Mrs. Simmons' body went limp as she reached for the counter.

Lance grabbed the frail woman and guided her to his chair.

"The brownies…my secret ingredient is peanut butter. I gave her a batch the day before…I didn't know…how would I know?" She began to wail.

"Is there someone we can call for you, ma'am?" asked Lance.

The woman took three long breaths before she could speak. "Yes, I need to call my nephew, Lanny. He's been in Texas on business since yesterday morning. I haven't had the heart to tell him about Cathy. He was leaving his wife because he and Cathy had fallen in love." She began to sob, again.

"Ma'am," said Charlie. "We need to ask you about the lottery tickets."

Mrs. Simmons sniffed twice, took off her glasses and wiped her face. "What on earth are you talking about?"

"Did you buy some lottery tickets a few days ago?"

"As a matter of fact, I did," she said. "I bought one for Lanny's birthday and Cathy had me buy one for her. She always bought the same numbers, you know. I had to write them down to make sure I got them right."

"Did you give the ticket to her?"

"Why, yes," she said. "I did. I gave her and Lanny their tickets at the same time I took her the brown –" She stopped in mid-sentence. "That was right before Lanny's wife showed up and made a scene."

"When was that, ma'am?"

"The night before Cathy died. You don't think Lanny had anything to do with…?"

"What's Lanny's last name, ma'am?"

"Fulton. Lanny Fulton."

* * *

Sherry Fulton wrinkled her nose and made a face. "This place stinks," she said. The jail cell smelled like bleach. She didn't much like the odor, but decided it was better than the alternative. There had been plenty of drunks, she was quite sure, spend their fair share of time inside this cage, puking and relieving themselves at their convenience.

"Talk to us, Sherry, and we'll find you a nicer place," said Charlie. "Officer Smith is interviewing your husband as we speak and since he just got here from out of town, I'm curious to see if your stories jibe."

Her shoulders shook as she began to speak. "That jerk. I caught him with her." She turned and looked at Charlie. "Not only that, she had already made friends with his aunt." She became quiet as if trying to decide whether to go on.

Charlie waited.

Finally, she began to speak again. "I knew she was allergic to peanuts. Lanny was always making a big deal about not buying anything containing peanuts. Finally, I figured out that peanuts didn't bother him at all. It was his new girlfriend. I found her prescription in his car about a week ago. When I realized what it was, I took it out and replaced the epinephrine with water. It was easy to do. I used to work as a clerk in a pharmacy and when they got behind, the pharmacist would let me help fill prescriptions."

A disapproving frown crossed Charlie's forehead.

"Anyway," she continued, "a few days ago I got fed up with his shenanigans and followed him to her house. I confronted them. She lived right next door to his aunt, mind you. Lanny asked me to leave and I did. But, I saw the brownies. Thought it was too good to be true. I knew how his aunt made them with peanut butter. You can't hardly taste it." She began to cry again. "I didn't think she would die, I just thought she would be miserable for a while. And I thought she deserved a little misery for stealing my husband." She placed her hands on her face and sobbed.

Charlie shook his head and motioned for the jailer to unlock the cell and let him out. He could still hear her sobs when he reached the end of the hall.

* * *

Gladys plopped a glass of ice water and an empty coffee mug on the counter in front of Charlie, then filled the cup with steaming brew. "So what did they charge her with?" she asked.

"Stupidity would have been my first choice," said Charlie, then tested the coffee with a cautious sip. "But the D.A.'s official charge is first degree manslaughter. I don't think she realized her little switch-a-roo would really kill the woman." He spooned some ice into his coffee. "I can't believe she won the lottery," he added.

"I don't get it," said Gladys. "What's all this got to do with her winning the lottery?"

"She won with the victim's numbers," said Charlie as he cradled the mug with his big hands. "According to the husband, when his aunt gave him and the Westerman girl their tickets, they got them mixed up. So, he ended up with his girlfriend's ticket. When he got home, he called her and they planned to exchange them when he got back from his trip. But, the wife found the ticket, checked the numbers and well, you know the rest."

"Heck of a way to win a lottery," said Gladys. "What happens to the money?"

"I guess you could say the husband is the winner…and the loser all at the same time. But, the good news is, he's got a dog that knows to bark when he sees a jar of peanut butter," said Charlie as he grinned.

"A lot of good that'll do him now." Gladys shook her head as she delivered a glass of ice water and a menu to the next customer.

~

Clandestine Meeting

by Moira K. Wiley

Hemlock my coy mistress
Twilight prophetically
Murmuring whispers
Through the trees

Mortified motionless
Tension rising while
Witnessing primeval acts
Realizing life's possibilities

Heart besieged
With pain and grief
Wingless creature
Begging for flight

Rigid back
With everlasting denial
Forgiveness eternally
Begging for sunlight

Our clandestine meeting
Proved fatal

Moira K. Wiley is the youngest member to ever serve as OWFI president. Her energetic ambition led her to quit her day job and plunge into freelancing when she found exactly what she looked for – the words Writer Wanted in the newspaper want ads. She has served as reporter for *Stillwater NewsPress*, editor for *GatorTales* and is the major contributing writer for *Emu Today and Tomorrow.* Some of her poetry, with a mysterious slant, can be found in the pages of *Almostly Murder... With Pets.*

~

Old Mack Donald's Ghost

by Moira K. Wiley

The gunshot was heard just before dawn, reverberating across the sleeping countryside and breaking the silence on Old Mack Donald's farm. The tranquil Monday morning, which usually found Old Mack toiling away, instead found the old farmer dead. Within the hour, the once peaceful farm was swarming with police officers, the county coroner and one detective.

Detective Kathryn Webb was considered an "old pro" in the homicide department and was immediately assigned the case. She had been with the department for ten years, but at 32, she was still the youngest detective at the Sixth Precinct in Sherwood, Oklahoma.

Kathryn had always known she wanted to be a cop. Her father was a cop, all three of her older brothers were cops, two of her three uncles were cops and her grandfather had been a county sheriff for 30 years until his retirement. Her mother died giving birth to Kathryn, and being raised by her father and three rambunctious, over-protective brothers only made her want to join the boys in blue more. She joined the police academy on her 21st birthday, much to her father's disapproval. He didn't like the idea of his only daughter putting herself in harm's way. After graduating from the police academy at the top of her class, Kathryn applied for a position in Sherwood, two counties away from where her father and brothers were stationed. She put in her time as a beat cop and was offered a detective's position three short years later.

Kathryn had worked several homicide cases, but she arrived on the scene that morning puzzled over why anyone would want to murder the kind old farmer whom she'd known since she first arrived in Sherwood. Old Mack brought fresh vegetables to the precinct every other Monday, because he felt the officers didn't eat right. So in Sherwood, instead of donut jokes, the cops had to contend with veggie jokes. As she passed one of her fellow officers Kathryn smiled sadly, both knowing they would never again hear Mack's cheerful greeting, "It's veggie day," as he lugged his basketful of vegetables through the precinct.

Why would anyone want to kill such a sweet, old man? she silently asked herself. Kathryn shook off her melancholy as she made her way over to the coroner.

"Hey Jake, got a cause and time of death for me?"

Jacob O'Bannon, the county's coroner, had been trying to get her to go out with him for years. He was an attractive, athletic 35-year-old man and she knew he had no problem getting dates, but he didn't want to date just anybody. Kathryn had his heart whether she wanted it or not. Unfortunately, she was so wrapped up in her career, proving a woman could do the job just as well as any man that she wasn't interested in getting romantically involved with anyone. The two had, however, become really good friends over the years and because Kathryn chose not to date and Jacob stopped dating when he fell for Kathryn, neither of them had to deal with the jealousy of seeing the other out with someone else.

"It wasn't too difficult to figure out," Jake replied professionally, barely masking the attraction he felt for the petite, auburn-haired detective. "He's got a clean shot to the chest with a large caliber pistol. The powder burns on his clothing indicate the shot was fired point blank. As to time of death, his widow and everyone within a mile heard the shot about six this morning and from my quick exam, I can see that the bullet pierced his heart killing him instantly. I guess that's the only good news I have for you is that he didn't suffer."

"Well, that's at least something," Kathryn replied.

"Of course, I'll still do a full autopsy at the morgue and have my report to you later this evening."

"I'd appreciate it," she said turning to a nearby officer and missing the longing look Jake threw her way. "Do you know who was first on the scene?" she asked.

"Yeah, Raines," the officer replied.

Kathryn groaned inwardly at the news. She and Raines didn't see eye to eye and hadn't since she'd been made detective seven years ago instead of him. She looked over her shoulder and exchanged a meaningful glance with Jake. His saying, *Sorry, your day just keeps getting better*, and hers saying, *Could it get any worse?*

"Hey, Webb, did you know there's a big, ugly bird in your car squawking at the top of its lungs, 'Step away from the vehicle, step away from the vehicle'?" asked the new rookie doing his best parrot impersonation.

"Brilliant detective work, Jones! I had no idea there was a bird in my car," Kathryn replied. She was being sarcastic, but everyone, including the rookie was used to that.

"What's with the bird," Jake asked.

"It's my friend's parrot. Damn thing keeps yanking out its own feathers. Stupid bird is half bald and very high-strung."

"So...what are you doing with it?"

"She had to go out of town for a couple of weeks on some business trip. She asked me to take the bird home because she was afraid to leave it at her house with its current feather fetish. Her flight left early this morning, and I had just picked up the bird when I got the call to come here and didn't have time to drop it off anywhere."

Jake started to chuckle. "Let me guess, you're going to let it ride on your shoulder and start wearing a patch over your eye?"

"Very funny. If you'll excuse me, I've got work to do," she said glaring, but her accompanying smirk told him she wasn't really mad.

"Yes ma'am, squawk," replied Jake giving his best parrot imitation.

Kathryn giggled in spite of herself.

"If you two are through flirting, I believe there's been a murder that needs to be solved."

Kathryn turned to face Raines' sneering face. Gritting her teeth, she put on her fakest smile and said, "Hey Raines, I was just coming to look for you. I hear you were the first one on the scene and have all the answers I'll need to solve this case."

"Don't give me that bull," he shot back. "I know you can't stand the thought of having to talk to me, so just drop the silly smile and let's get down to business."

"Whatever you say. What do you have for me?" Kathryn replied, silly smile still in place.

Raines rolled his eyes. "So far, not much."

"Really…." she replied with feigned shock.

"I'm warning you, smart aleck…."

"OK, OK. I'm sorry, please continue," Kathryn said, trying to get serious and quit intentionally trying to provoke the burly officer.

"I've had officers searching the grounds, but so far all we have are a couple sets of footprints that don't seem to belong to Mack or anyone associated with his farm. We haven't found the murder weapon or anything else that might indicate who or why the crime was committed."

"OK, I'll take over from here," she replied. "Any officer who is not a trained detective needs to leave. I don't want there to be any chance of a piece of evidence getting ruined because some overly ambitious, inexperienced beat cop can't pay attention to where he's walking."

"Listen to Miss High and Mighty," Raines spat. "You forget that you were once an overly ambitious, inexperienced beat cop yourself at one time. Now, you just waltz in here thinking you're the best detective since Columbo."

Kathryn started laughing so hard tears came to her eyes.

"What's so damn funny?" yelled Raines.

"Columbo...Columbo...." She couldn't catch her breath long enough to get out what she was trying to say.

"Yeah, that's what I said – Columbo," Raines said getting more puzzled by the minute. "I think you've finally gone over the edge, Webb."

Kathryn took a deep breath and tried to still her laughter. "The stupid bird in my car is named Columbo. When my friend found him in the pet shop, he was already named. The shop owner said he couldn't get enough of old detective and cop shows, which was how he got his name. It's also the reason he spouts off police jargon.

"The other night I stopped by my friend's house after work, and when I took my gun off to get comfortable, Columbo starts squawking, 'Drop your weapon, squawk. Put your hands above your head, squawk,' at the top of his lungs over and over. I nearly wet myself, I laughed so hard."

Everyone within earshot of the story was chuckling pretty hard themselves. Kathryn had done a pretty good parrot imitation herself, but Raines was not impressed with her witty story at his expense.

"How amusing," Raines replied sarcastically with a look conveying his feeling that she was a complete loser. "If you're through relating a night in the life of the exciting Detective Webb, I have work to do back at the station."

Unfazed, Kathryn replied, "Then, by all means, I won't keep you any longer. Take the rest of these guys with you."

"I'm not your lapdog. Clear your own crime scene," Raines sneered one last time, then turned and stalked off in the direction where his cruiser was parked.

"I really dislike that guy," Kathryn said to nobody in particular.

"Just dislike? I'm sure you can do better than that, Kat," Jake replied.

Jake was the only person other than her dad she allowed to call her Kat. She didn't know why she didn't mind hearing the nickname come from his lips when it irritated her so much from anyone else.

"Yeah, well hate is such a strong emotion, and he's not worth the time or the energy," she replied.

"Yeah, those damn emotions are so time consuming. Too bad you couldn't at least try one on for size every once in a while," Jake replied a bit peevishly and walked away.

"What was that all about?" Kathryn asked herself. Shrugging off her confusion, she set about starting her investigation.

She went back to her car to get her kit, which included the items she'd need to get castings of the footprints the officers had found. She stuck her head in her open driver-side window and grabbed the kit out of her backseat.

"Dust for fingerprints, squawk. Dust for fingerprints, squawk."

"Thanks for the tip, Columbo," she said smiling at the parrot.

Kathryn worked all through the afternoon and into the evening. She walked the grounds searching for any scrap of evidence that would point a finger at the person who killed the kind farmer. Her back was starting to ache and her stomach rumbled loudly when she noticed she was losing the sun as it slowly set in the west.

She rubbed her stomach in a feeble attempt to still the hunger pangs. "Come on, stomach. Work with me. I still haven't found what I'm looking for."

Her answer was another loud grumble.

"OK, you win. Let me check out this last paddock over here and we'll go get something to eat and start again in the morning. There's not much light left anyway," she said and then laughed. "I can't believe I'm having a conversation with my stomach."

Still chuckling, she grabbed the flashlight she carried in her kit and switched it on. She opened the six-foot gate on the pen located in a remote back corner of the farmer's vast property and started her search as the sun disappeared, cloaking the countryside in darkness.

At that moment, Kathryn felt a sharp pain in her right earlobe. "Ouch! What the...?" She spun around trying to see in the dark and rubbing her ear. She shined the flashlight's beam to the left and slowly to the right. She had almost decided that a bee or something like that must have stung her and started to turn back to her task when she saw a white apparition in the distance turn and head towards her.

"What is that?" she asked aloud. The ghost-like object was quickly closing in and Kathryn was backing as quickly as she could to the spot she thought the gate was located and unsheathed her Beretta 9mm from the holster inside her jacket.

She aimed at the translucent being that was now within 50 feet of her and she still couldn't make out anything but a white shape. "I don't believe in ghosts, so what the heck is that?" She asked herself aloud while feeling behind her for the gate that she was sure was there.

"Seeing ghosts are we?" said a voice out of the darkness.

Kathryn spun around, gun in hand and collided soundly into Jake O'Bannon.

"Hey, watch that piece of yours. It's just me, Jake. You're awfully jumpy." He quickly identified himself before she accidentally put a bullet in him. He placed one of his hands on her shoulder as he spoke trying to convey he was a friend.

"Oh," replied Kathryn and then spun back around to find the "ghost," tripping over her own feet in her haste. Jake stepped closer, wrapping his arms around her to break her fall. She landed with a dull thud against his broad chest, and he pulled her tightly against him on the pretense of helping her regain her balance. She was half twisted, leaning against Jake with his arms locked firmly around her waist, but her gun hand was free and targeting the apparition she could just make out by the light of the moon that had stopped some 30 feet away.

"Easy, Dirty Harry. Don't fire, it's not a ghost and if it was, a bullet wouldn't do much good, now would it," Jake said teasingly close to her ear. He reached out, placed his hand over hers and slowly lowered her arm to her side. The whole while he kept his grip around her tiny waist and held her as close as the awkward position would allow. Throwing caution to the wind, he nuzzled her ear with his nose, breathing in her scent.

Kathryn sucked in her breath and her eyes closed of

their own accord. Suddenly, she lunged out of his arms and turned around to face him from a safe distance away.

"What are you doing here?" she asked accusingly.

"Get out of detective mode, Kat. I went down to the precinct to give you my autopsy report and they said you hadn't made it back in. I assumed you were still here, so I drove on out, and the rest is history," he replied playfully.

"You could have left it on my desk," she said crossly.

"What's the big deal, Kat? So, you liked me holding you. That's a normal reaction when a woman likes the man whose arms are around her."

"I'm not going through this again, Jake. I told you I don't have time for – Ouch!" Kathryn cried out as she felt a pain in her earlobe again. She spun around with flashlight and gun raised and came face to face, so to speak, with what looked like Big Bird from Sesame Street.

"He likes your earrings," Jake said.

"What is it?" Kathryn asked, as the bird tried to circle around behind her, but she followed it step for step until it was between the couple.

"It's an emu," Jake said, patting it on the back as he stepped around the large bird to join her on the other side. "You know, flightless bird from Australia, looks like a big chicken, tastes like beef and very popular alternative livestock."

"I know what an emu is," Kathryn replied testily. "But, they have ugly brown and gray feathers, this thing is white and looks like a damn ghost."

"There are some rare cases of emus that have blonde or, in this case, white feathers," Jake explained. "The pain you felt was it trying to get your earring. They like shiny stuff and those diamond studs of yours shine really well in this moonlight."

"What is a white emu doing here?"

"Actually, Mack has two," Jake explained. "This one is

male and there's a bigger one that's female. They're a breeding pair and very valuable. He was always turning people away who wanted to buy the pair. He sold every egg the female ever laid to some researcher over in Australia."

"Wow, I never knew that," Kathryn said, relaxing her stance. She gingerly reached one hand out until she was touching the giant bird. He seemed to be enjoying the attention until something caught his eye behind her, and he nearly knocked her over as he pushed past to get a closer look.

"Stupid bird!" Kathryn complained and turned to see what had caught the emu's eye. Lights, there were lights flashing around the wooded area that bordered the back part of the property where the pen was located.

"Who would be out here in the middle of the night?" Kathryn asked and then quickly flipped the switch on her flashlight to the off position, so whoever was sneaking up the back way wouldn't see it. "Well, I know that can't be Old Mack, and his wife went to stay with relatives," she said, keeping her voice low, so it wouldn't carry. "Hey Jake, get over there behind that shed while I go find out who that is."

"Ah, afraid I might get hurt? I didn't know you cared," he whispered back in a teasing tone of voice.

"Get moving, wise guy," she replied and stealthily made her way along the fence line keeping her eye on the two flashing beams that were now making their way across the field.

She could hear two voices arguing heatedly, both male and definitely headed her way.

"It's stupid to come back here so soon," one yelled.

"No, it's the perfect time. Everyone is gone, and no one would expect anyone to come out here tonight since the old guy got shot this morning."

"Yeah, well, I don't know why you had to shoot him in

the first place."

"Shut up! I told you it was an accident. What were we supposed to do? He caught us trying to steal those emus and was on his way to call the cops. I tried to reason with him, but he just kept getting closer to the house, even when I waved the gun in his face. Stupid, old man! Why couldn't he have just sold us those emus?"

Kathryn had heard all she needed. These two were responsible for Old Mack's death and all over two rare birds that he refused to sell. They were nearly on top of her, so she flattened herself next to what felt like a large corner post, hoping they were too immersed in their argument to notice her.

As they passed by her in her makeshift hiding spot, she came up directly behind them with her gun ready and said, "Police! Don't move! You're surrounded! Lay face down on the ground with your hands above your head."

Both men yelped and immediately fell to the ground. She quickly stuffed the gun in the back of her jeans, grabbed her handcuffs and got the first man cuffed. Luckily, her eyes had adjusted to the dark enough to see what she was doing. Realizing she only had one pair of handcuffs, she began searching around for something she could use to tie up the other guy when Jake appeared holding a long piece of rope.

"I thought I told you to stay behind that shed," she accused.

"I thought you might need some backup," he replied sheepishly.

"You're not a trained police officer and could have really gotten yourself hurt," she replied angrily as she snatched the rope out of his hand and tied up the second man.

"So, you do care what happens to me," he teased.

"You are my friend. Since when am I not allowed to

care about what happens to a friend?" Kathryn snapped as she stood to face him now that both men were securely bound.

Jake grabbed her around the waist, yanked her into his arms and tried to look into her eyes in the darkness. "You just can't admit that you could be attracted to me, can you?" And with that comment, he unerringly put his lips over hers and kissed her soundly. "When you get done taking these two into the station and filling out your report, why don't you come by my house. I think it's about time we discussed our feelings for each other like two adults."

He gently released her and headed towards his car. As she watched him go, Kathryn tried to slow her breathing and quiet her rapidly beating heart. She took a deep breath, held it for a count of ten and then let it out on a sigh. Trying to shake off the desire that had inflamed her with Jake's kiss, she went about collecting her prisoners, so she could head to the station.

At the station, everyone was impressed that Kathryn had caught the two would-be emu rustlers and patted her on the back for capturing the guy who had murdered Old Mack. Kathryn half listened to their compliments, still thinking about that kiss.

"Yeah, lucky for me they came in the back way or they might have seen my car and that stupid parrot would have probably said something like, 'Stop in the name of the law, squawk,'" she said making a feeble attempt at humor.

Even Raines begrudgingly threw her a "good job" as she passed his desk, but Kathryn couldn't even work up enough interest to gloat. All she could think about was how good it had felt to have Jake's lips on hers, so she officially relinquished her prisoners and headed out the front door without a backward glance. She smiled as she came to the realization that being a great detective didn't mean she couldn't also be a woman, and Jake was waiting for her.

Conversation with a Corpse

by Moira K. Wiley

Dead men can tell tales
Skin left under fingernails
A hair, carpet fiber or other scrap
Can all lead to a murder rap

Bloodstains on a sleeve
Evidence, the crime can leave
Fingerprints found with dust
For homicide, can mean a bust

Forensic science, a killer's foe
Real work, not just for show
Detectives digging for clues
Justice wins, murderers lose

Murderous Intent

by Moira K. Wiley

Clearly noting your
Murderous intent
    My days on earth
    Are already spent
        Mayhem gleaming
        Behind evil eyes
            Never should I believe
            Your little lies
                Stained knife wielded
                With explicit malice
                    Blood you'll drink
                    From your chalice
                        Gazing through the flies
                        Looking back with dead eyes

M. E. Cooper at one time wanted to be the Dick Francis of motorcycle racing. She loves a good adventure and writes great action scenes and fast plots. In this story she slows the pace and shows her talent as an eclectic writer who can fit her style to the story. Readers should get a chill out of this one.

~

Inuit Traditions

by M. E. Cooper

Everything about the man was brown, from his skin to his hair, to his rather sleazy suit. Even the watchband on his left wrist was brown leather. I don't usually take an instant dislike to people but there was something about him I found immediately distasteful.

I glanced at my daughter and saw from the tiny crease between her eyebrows and the cold regard in her eyes that she was no more attracted to him than I was. His voice was oily, unctuous, or as the English would say it, 'smarmy' sounding.

He explained that the director of the Evergreen Nursing Home had given him our names. The director had no business telling this creature anything about us.

Oblivious to our disapproval, Mr. Andrews continued his sales spiel. Evidently he thought by buttering us up we would be more receptive, because he began to heap compliments on the furnishings of the house, the grounds, the lovely garden, etc.

Alicia glanced at me, smoothed her skirt and I knew she had had her fill of this. She was ready to make an exit, leaving me alone with this odious sales person.

I begged her with my eyes not to leave, so she settled back against the chair. Alicia has achieved remarkable success in her career, especially since she is not yet forty, but I also know she does not suffer fools gladly. I would have to take the initiative and get rid of this pest or listen to him drone on for hours alone.

"Just what exactly is Inuit Traditions, Mr. Andrews? What is it you are trying to sell us?"

"Dear ladies, I am prepared to solve all your problems. Our company is founded on the past, on ancient practices and traditions."

Alicia raised her eyebrows and looked at me with no more understanding than I had myself.

"What precisely are you talking about?"

"Let me speak frankly, if I may. You have an elderly mother who is a burden. In all likelihood she will require years of nursing home care. To provide for her care, you will be forced to sell this lovely home of hers to use the proceeds for her needs."

I found my hands clenching in my lap. Although I should be used to it, I always feel as if I'm being slapped in the face when someone reminds me that due to a disastrous marriage I was left with no retirement, except for a pittance of social security income.

Alicia looked over at me with sympathy, but then focused her gaze on the brown man. "Are you suggesting a cheaper nursing home?"

"Oh, no, no, no. Dear Ladies, there is only one solution for a situation like this. A permanent, quick solution."

"Like Doctor Kervorkian, perhaps?" Alicia's voice was sarcastic.

His smile made me feel even more uneasy. "Nothing that crude, nothing at all like that. You see in the Inuit tradition, elders are given every consideration. You simply explain to your mother that you are taking her on a luxurious trip to Alaska. I have some brochures right here for you to show her." He handed each of us a trifold, glossy, colorful travel pamphlet.

"After your arrival at our destination, we will make your mother comfortable with tranquilizers and some hot toddies to drink. Then she will be taken out by dog sled to the edge of a glacier, where she will be lulled by telling her that it is a uniquely Alaskan experience to view the night sky.

"In twenty minutes, the extreme cold will affect her nervous system. There is no suffering, no pain at all. A little shivering, yes, but that quickly passes. Voila, in a relatively short time, we will return the body to your hotel, where our doctor will certify death by natural causes. Then you may arrange transport home for burial, or you might wish to partake of our crematorium there."

I was so stunned by the outrageous suggestion, I could only stare at the man. Alicia, however, seemed interested.

"How much?"

He named a figure which made me gasp, but he quickly explained, "Remember that is only a fraction of what you'll be realizing from the inheritance."

"I think we should discuss this alone for a moment." Alicia strode from the room, with me following her.

"You're not actually seriously considering this?" I protested.

"Well, now, Mom. Let's not be too hasty to dismiss the idea. I admit at first I thought the man was a sleaze, but there are definitely some positive benefits to this plan. You know yourself that Gram is becoming more and more of a problem. You're wearing yourself out visiting the nursing home to see a drooling, incontinent, old woman. Wouldn't it be nice if she was out of the way and we could just enjoy life?"

The idea was certainly tempting, but I still felt reluctant to employ such drastic means. "I can understand when patients ask for assisted suicide, but Mother isn't asking to be released from life. I just don't see how we can do such a thing!"

"When Gram was herself, would she have wanted to be a burden?"

"Well, no. She was a very unselfish woman. In fact, she insisted I come live here because it's so much nicer than my tiny little furnished apartment."

"So you see that this is really what she would have wanted. I'm certain you should sign up for the trip."

When Alicia stared at me like that, I felt my resistance crumbling. We argued for a time, but finally I could see her mind was made up. Timidly, I asked, "Would you be willing to go with us to Alaska?"

"Of course." Alicia was briskly efficient. "I'll have to make arrangements to take my vacation early, but that won't be a problem."

Feeling tremulous, I followed her out of the room, back to where Mr. Andrews waited with his brochures of Alaska.

Since I was her next of kin with power of attorney, Mr. Andrews handed me the pen to sign all the numerous, lengthy forms. When I couldn't do it, Alicia took the pen out of my hands, saying briskly, "I'll sign your name, Mom, to spare you any discomfort." A short time later, all the forms were signed, so she left quickly.

Everything concerning the trip went unbelievably well. There were no snags on our flight or our check-in at the hotel. I was so nervous about taking my mother out on the ice floe, that I gratefully accepted the hot toddy Alicia offered me. In fact, it wasn't until I saw the two chairs out on the ice that I understood. Speechless with shock, I stared at Mr. Andrews and my daughter.

As Alicia calmly patted the lead dog's head, he said, "Don't be alarmed. You won't suffer long, if at all. It is the tradition."

~

Fate

by Rey Hanan

One of my best friends was struck down by a hit and run driver on a lonely road outside Albuquerque, New Mexico.

He had been missing for about a month. His body was found in a ditch beside the road, hidden in the tall weeds. I found the body.

On a whim, that morning, I had decided to go out to the Indian Reservation to buy my sister a turquoise necklace for her birthday. On the way home, I saw an odd looking pile of rubbish in the ditch. I slammed on the brakes, jumped out of the car, and ran over to the area for a better look. It was him! My beautiful, black, French poodle. He hadn't been dead long. Crying all the while, I looked around for something to carry him home in. As fate would have it, not ten feet away was a small, new cardboard box. I lifted him into the box, put him on the passenger seat, and we went home.

My husband dug a grave in our backyard, and we invited our sons and their wives to a simple burial ceremony. I gave the eulogy and the others spoke of the memories they had when Beau was a puppy. My husband and I went out on the mesa and got a large smooth rock for his headstone. I painted on it:

Beau Hanan
May 1975 – August 1985

~

Rey Hanan, a.k.a. Rachelle Hanan, first of all is a prize-winning professional artist and gained membership in the National League of American Pen Women through her art. Through her efforts a Pen Women chapter was established in Stillwater, Oklahoma. She is a storyteller, letters-to-the-editor writer and prize-winning cherry pie baker. She loves to read and took up writing to explore other creative venues.

~

Pride Goeth

by Rey Hanan

A Siamese cat sat unmoving atop the dressing table next to the bottles of expensive cologne. Her head was turned toward the loud and angry voices of the other occupants.

"What do you think you're doing? How dare you try to cuddle up to me? We put on an act in public, not in my bedroom. My friends think we have a marriage made in heaven. I can't let them know we have a marriage made in hell. Now, get out of my room. I have my pride, you know. Get out!"

The cat just sat there. Her slightly crossed blue eyes never blinked.

"Myra, please, don't be so vicious. We can make a go of our marriage. I'm not a crook. I'm actually a pretty good guy. I've never killed anyone."

"You've killed me spiritually. I might as well be dead as to pretend I'm happy all the time. You don't know how I hate the play acting we do in front of my friends. If I only had the words."

The cat looked on.

"You're doing a pretty good job of insulting me with the words you have. I haven't done anything unforgivable. You knew I liked to drink when you married me. I wanted to wait, but oh, no, you insisted we marry immediately. Now, you'll just have to put up with me if you won't give me a divorce. It's your pride. You're miserable because of your damn pride. And make your damn cross-eyed cat stop glaring at me."

"Poor little Jezebel. Did that mean old man talk naughty about you?" Myra picked up the cat and stroked her head. "Jezebel can't help it if her beautiful blue eyes are crossed." The cat tried to escape, but Myra held on tight.

He unbuttoned his shirt and loosened his tie. "We can go on living like this. It doesn't matter to me. It isn't costing me anything."

"You're so disgusting. Get out of my room!"

"OK, I'm going. Before I forget, are we scheduled to make a public appearance this evening? I'd like to make a few plans of my own."

"I'm staying home," she said, staring into the mirror above the array of cosmetics and perfume bottles.

"Thank you, my dear. You make me happy, even when you don't mean to." As Kirk was leaving the bedroom, Jezebel yowled and leaped from Myra's arms, streaking out of the open door.

Myra hates me and I hate her. Maybe too much. He walked heavily out of the house, then slid behind the wheel of his Porsche.

* * *

"Kirk, darling. I was beginning to think you had forgotten our date."

"Would I forget a thing like that? I'm sorry I'm late. I had some last minute problems. How's my girl?"

"Fine, now that you're here. Kirk, I'm always afraid you will walk out of here some night and never come back. Darling, promise me you won't ever do that to me."

"I promise. Word of honor. You worry too much. Let's have a drink."

"Kirk."

"Yes?"

"Sometimes I think you drink too much."

"Oh, my God! Not you, too!"

"Someone else has accused you of drinking too much? I don't understand. Who? Kirk, I wish you would tell me more about yourself."

"Don't worry about it. Come here and give me a great big kiss and then go fix me that drink I asked for. Pretty, please."

Bess walked over to Kirk, flung her arms around his neck and gave a passionate, loving kiss. "I wish I could refuse you anything." She left to make him a drink.

Even being here with Bess, doesn't keep me from thinking of Myra. I want out. I have to decide what to do. Myra is the thorn in my side. Myra has a tad too much money and a tad too much pride. However, when I think about it, why should I want to get rid of her? She keeps me in the style to which I have become accustomed. I can't afford to lose her. We will just have to go along as we are. Beggars can't be choosy. Spending a few romantic hours with Bess is pleasant, but not exactly earth shattering. Oh well, here's Bess with my drink.

"Thank you for a wonderful evening. You are so sweet and loving. It's time I get home. Duty calls, my day starts early. Give me a big kiss and then I'm out of here. Bye, Babe, see ya."

Kirk got into his car, started the motor, just as a furry ball leaped from the back seat, over his shoulder and landed in the passenger seat.

"What the hell? Where did you come from? Jezebel, how did you get in my car? Are you spying on me?" *I suppose you're going to report back to Myra. I can nip that in the bud. I can put you out right here and make you find your own way home. I can't believe I'm talking to a damn cross-eyed cat. It's a relief to know that she won't talk back. Wouldn't surprise me though, all females are alike. Blah, blah,blah.*

"Kirk, I was wondering when you would finally get home. Tomorrow we're going to the Culvers for cocktails. Break all your engagements. I'll expect you to be ready by eight. Wear your navy blue suit. It will compliment my blue gown."

"Yes, dear. I'm always happy to do just as you demand." He pretended to salute.

"Oh, stop being sarcastic. I hate it when you're pretending to be cooperative. Just be yourself. That's the one I can't stand."

"Now, you have me confused. I'm beginning to think you don't like me, when everyone knows I'm your devoted husband. You might be interested in knowing that I don't give a big rat's ass whether you like me or not."

"Just be ready by eight. I almost forgot to ask. Have you seen Jezebel? She hasn't touched her food today. I hope nothing has happened to her."

The reason you haven't seen Jezebel is because she was hiding in my car. I can't live much longer like this. Constant bickering, constant degrading comments about me, to me. I used to be a man. She has got to go. I wish I had the nerve to just finish her off. I wish there was a way, a perfect way to be rid of her.

Later, Myra called out, "Kirk it's almost eight. Time to go. Bring the car around. I wonder where that Jezebel could be?" The ride to the Culvers' was in complete silence. When they arrived, Myra waited for Kirk to come around and open her door, before she would put one foot out.

"Oh, for God's sake. Get out of the car, nobody is spying on us." Kirk stomped around to the passenger's side and opened the door.

"Give me your arm. Escort me to the door like a true gentlemen."

"Yes, your highness. Is it all right if I ring the doorbell?"

The door opened and a blonde with a shrill voice greeted them. "Myra, darling. I'm so glad you could come. We always love to have the 'perfect couple' as our guests. I'm so envious of you two lovebirds."

Envious! If she only knew! I wonder if Myra has changed her will? I'll have to check on that before I make a move.

"Amy Culver, what a nice thing to say! Anyone can have a marriage like Kirk and mine. You just have to work at it."

Work is right. I have never seen anyone work as hard at anything as Myra does to make people think we are the happiest couple in the universe. Hey, that's good. No one will ever suspect me, a loving and devoted husband. Myra would have made a damn good actress. I almost hate to have anything happen to her.

"Kirk, you haven't said a word." Myra playfully jabbed his cheek with her finger. "Sweetheart, tell Amy how glad we are to have been asked to her lovely party."

"Amy, it's nice to be asked to your lovely party.

Besides, Amy, you serve the best damn liquor in the county. Thanks for inviting us."

"Kirk, you are so cute."

Cute! I can't stand that woman, either. Her voice is like fingernails on a blackboard. Thank God I'm not married to her, because I'd kill her without any plan. There must be a perfect way to get rid of my wife. Gun. Shot through the head..suicide...no...strangled? No, that would leave purple marks on her neck and Myra would be upset if her neck were discolored. Forensic science would come after me in a New York minute. It will have to be poison. But what kind of poison? I don't have a clue.

"Kirk, you look like you're a million miles away."

"Oh, sorry. What did you say?"

"What will you have to drink?"

"Whiskey, straight, please."

"Kirk, this party won't last that long and then you can have Myra all to yourself. You'll have to wait until the first guest leaves though. You owe Myra that much. Just be patient." Amy's smile was lecherous.

He gritted his teeth, hoping it looked like a grin. "Amy, stop. You're making me blush."

"That will be the day. You haven't blushed since you were six years old." Amy beckoned to the maid and told her to bring Myra some white wine and Kirk some whiskey straight.

While sipping his whiskey, Kirk contemplated his problems. *Damn. I forgot all about Bess. What am I going to do with her? What a mess! Is this damn party going to last forever? I have to go by and see Bess, before she starts gnashing her teeth. Oh, good. The Greene's are leaving. It's about time. Myra and I can be right behind them.*

"Myra, dear, are you ready to leave?"

"Be with you in a minute. I want to finish telling Amy about the beautiful bracelet you gave me."

Kirk hoped he didn't look shocked. *Sometimes she even surprises me! Lies and more lies. It will be a cold day in hell before I spend any money on a bracelet for her.*

They drove home in silence. "I'm glad we're finally home. I thought that party would last all night. I'm sorry, Myra, but I have to go out."

She flipped her purse over her arm angrily, "Good riddance. Stay as long as you like. Who cares?"

* * *

"Bess, where are you?" Kirk went through the house calling. He found her in the bedroom. "What in the world at you doing in bed at this time of evening? Bess! Bess! My God, Bess wake up! What the hell?" Glancing down he saw an empty bottle of sleeping pills. *I wonder how many she swallowed? I've got to get her up on her feet and walk her.* "Damn it Bess, stand up! I can't do this alone."

Walk, walk, back and forth. I wonder how many of the sleeping pills she swallowed? And why? Should I call 911?

"Bess, wake up!"

"Kirk?"

"Bess, keep walking. Try harder. Damn it, Bess, walk. Why did you take those sleeping pills?"

"Because I can't go on like this. This is the end."

"You don't know what you're saying. Keep walking. You had better have a damn good reason or doing such a damn fool stunt! I can't stand neurotic women. Keep walking."

"Kirk, I'm pregnant. I'm going to have a baby! You have to marry me!"

"Baby! Oh my God! That's all I need. How could you let that happen? A baby! Keep walking. I can't marry you, I'm already married."

"You're married? Kirk, you're married and you have

been coming here? Telling me you love me? I've felt all along that I couldn't trust you."

"My wife doesn't understand me. She doesn't care what I do, so why should I tell you about my other life?"

"Then get a divorce."

"No can do. My wife won't give me a divorce."

"You had better change her mind!" Bess seemed to have recovered totally from her sleeping pill induced haze. Her eyes were sharp as she snarled, "If you think I'm going to give birth to a bastard kid, you're crazy. That's why I took the sleeping pills. I knew you were a good for nothing skirt chaser. You should have let me go on sleeping forever."

He reached out for her, smoothing her hair and putting his hands on her shoulders. Staring into her eyes. he said, "Now you're being dramatic. We'll think of something. Don't worry."

"Don't worry!" She twisted out of his hands. "Walking me up and down and telling me everything is going to fine is a load of crap. Who do you think you're fooling? Not me, buster! I'm going to get married and guess who the groom is going to be. You'll just have to get rid of the little woman and I'll give you a week to do it, before I squeal."

Kirk ran a hand through his hair. "A week isn't long enough. I have a lot of things to work out. I need more time." *She doesn't understand that Myra holds the money. If I try to walk out immediately, I walk away with nothing.*

"A week and no longer! I'm not going to get married when I'm as big as an elephant, I don't care what Hollywood stars are doing. I have my pride, you know."

"Don't ever use that word *Pride* again. I hate that word! Now go to bed and get some rest. How many sleeping pills did you take anyway?"

When she didn't answer, he said, "Not enough apparently. You probably didn't take enough to harm the baby. I'll be back tomorrow."

Narrowing her eyes, she warned, "Kirk, just one last word. If you haven't figured out something about this problem in a week's time, I'm going to visit your wife."

Of all the damn things to have happen! I have to talk to Myra's lawyer. I hope she hasn't changed her will. I've got to get rid of her. I guess it will have to be either drugs or poison. Gotta make it look like something other than murder. Who would want to murder Myra besides me? Cops always suspect the spouse. No one else would suspect me, since I've got such a reputation of being such a loving husband.

Bess sure surprised me tonight. She's a lot tougher than I thought. Why should I marry her? She's a big girl now. And she's been around the block a few times. A baby! What if she goes to Myra? I gotta do something fast. I wonder if it would be too suspicious if they both turned up dead?

His thoughts seemed to run around his brain like a hamster on a treadmill. Five days later, his thoughts were no more coherent.

I can't believe almost a week has gone by. The only thing I have accomplished is to get the drug Veronal. The lady pharmacist was easy. A little pat here and there and she was ready to climb my bones. She forked over the stuff without any questions asked. I hope the encyclopedia was correct. It said the drug would affect the heart adversely.

Next problem. How do I administer the drug? I can't just walk up to her and suggest she swallow it. Imagine the look on her face. She would be too surprised to say, "I hate you." Hell, she would never be that shocked. I can't leave a clue as to how the drug was administered. Detectives always check for fingerprints and they always have the dregs in a glass analyzed. I wonder if Myra has changed her will. Getting the Veronal into Myra is a big pain-in-the-ass problem. I'll have to go to Bess and plead for more time. I can't have her telling Myra about the baby. Two days to solve this crap. It's impossible!

Later, facing his lover, Kirk said, "Bess, you'll have to give me more time. Everything is just about set."

Bess shook her head, crossing her arms in front of her.

Bess certainly had a funny look on her face when I asked for more time. She hasn't said much all evening. I wonder what she's thinking? I can't trust her, I know that!

"It's getting late, time for me to go. I sure enjoyed being with you this evening."

"Yeah, I'll bet you did." Bess seemed not as loving as she usually was.

"Gotta go. Take care." He gave her a quick kiss on the cheek.

"You, too."

The next afternoon, he heard a command. "Kirk, come in here!"

Strolling into her bedroom, he asked, "What does my wonderful, loving wife wish to converse with me about?"

"Bess was here this morning."

"Bess! What in hell was she doing here?"

"She told me she is having a baby. Your baby. You are a disgrace. What do you intend to do about this unspeakable situation?"

"Bess insists I marry her. She wants you to give me a divorce."

Throwing down her hairbrush so hard it bounced off the dresser, she shouted, "No divorce! You'll have to come up with some other solution. I have gone to too much trouble to keep the secret of our pitiful marriage from my friends without the scandal of a skirt-chasing husband about to become the father of a bastard child. I shall not speak of this again! I'm not giving you a divorce, period. We are invited to the Matthews' for dinner this evening. I expect you to go. Be ready by seven. In the morning I will contact my lawyer."

I've got to do something tonight. Last chance. Damn, Bess. Why can't a woman believe just one thing I tell her? They are all alike. Bess had her nerve coming here. I asked for more time. She didn't say no, because she had already planned to come here. I won't marry her, that's for damn sure. Everything is piling up. I'm trapped, no escape. Tonight has to be the night to break free.

"Kirk, have you seen Jezebel lately? I am really concerned. I hope nothing has happened to her." When he just shook his head, she said, "You may go."

* * *

"Good evening, Norma. It was so nice for you to invite us to dinner. You always have such wonderful parties. All the guests are so interesting. Excuse me, there's Amy Culver. I must tell her a bit of gossip. Aren't we women atrocious? Gossip, gossip, gossip. And yet we're so sweet! Kirk, dear, do you want to come along or would you rather stay and chat with Norma?"

"I'd rather stay and chat with Norma. Norma, you look mighty fetching this evening. You are one of the few women I know who make sense to me."

"Darling Kirk, you always know just the right thing to say and when to say it. Myra is certainly a lucky girl and I might add, you are a lucky guy to have such a sweet and beautiful wife."

"Yes, I agree. Sometimes I think I don't appreciate Myra half enough. If anything should happen to her I don't know what I'd do. She has been to see her doctor. Something about her heart."

"Why, Kirk. I had no idea. I'm sorry. Is it serious?"

"Yes, it is, but she is very touchy about the idea of

being ill, so please don't ask her anything about her health. She gets very upset."

Norma patted his arm. "You're a brave boy! I promise not to say a word. I wouldn't want to upset her."

"Thank you, Norma. I'm looking forward to the dinner. Tonight I'm starved."

"Ah, perfect timing. Here's Hilda now. Shall we all go in?"

Tonight, I've got to do it tonight. Damn, I haven't much time left. I wish I could sit by Myra during dinner, but that's never the case. This capsule is going to be worn out before I get the damn thing down her. I must act natural. I think it was pretty smart of me to plant the idea of Myra's heart condition in Norma's delicate ear. She believed it! She called me a brave boy. I can count on her spreading the word when Myra keels over. I wish this dinner was over. Ah! Time to retire to the living room. All I need is a little bit of luck. I've got to sit by Myra to slip the capsule into her coffee. I believe the dinner went pretty well. No one seemed to think I was acting odd. I wonder if I answered all my dinner partner's stupid questions all right? What an idiot!

Kirk motioned to his wife, "Myra darling, come sit by me. I haven't talked to you all evening."

Amy's shrill voice echoed across the room, "There you go again, Kirk. I wish I could get my husband to dote on me the way you do Myra. He never says the sweet things your husband does."

Myra gave Amy a knowing smile, "Amy, how you exaggerate! Your husband adores you."

The doorbell rang, causing the conversation to cease. "I wonder who could be calling at this time of night?" As the maid came into the room, Norma said, "Yes, Hilda?"

"Mrs. Matthews, someone is here to speak to Mr. and Mrs. Allison."

"Did the person give a name?"

"A Miss Bess Dickens."

At those words, Myra turned deathly pale and slumped to the floor.

"Myra, darling! Myra! Are you all right? She's fainted. It must be her heart. Quick, someone. Get me a glass of water. Myra darling, speak to me." They were all milling around, offering suggestions. Some were watching Kirk. "Call 911!" He was sweating. "Dammit, get an ambulance here!"

Now, if I can get the damn capsule out of my pocket, put it between my lips, hold it with my teeth. Be calm. Lean over and pretend to give her the 'kiss of life'. Slowly slip the capsule between her parted teeth. Done! What a wonderful way to do someone in. No trace left on a cup, no glass, nothing left behind to point a finger toward me.

"Should you start CPR?" Norma asked.

"It's her heart. Myra, please open your eyes." *If she opens her eyes now, I'll die. Look at all the witnesses. Everyone is standing around staring at me. I must act very concerned.* "Here, sweetheart. Let me help you, just take a little sip of water to help revive you."

"Be careful, Kirk. You don't want Myra to choke."

"Did someone call the doctor?"

"Yes, an ambulance is on the way and he'll meet them at the hospital. I'm frightened for Myra. She looks so pale and still. She hasn't moved since she fainted."

The longer it takes the paramedics to get here, the longer I have for the Veronal to work. No one in this room even suspects that Myra will never move again, nor do they realize a murder was committed right before their eyes. I am so damn clever. No one else would have thought of inserting the capsule that way. I wonder what happened to Bess? I hope she had sense enough to leave. It would be just like her to stand around with her mouth wide open, instead of getting the hell out of there. I'm not going to worry about her. Damn, I'm glad that this is almost over now, so I can relax.

In the hospital emergency room, Kirk implored the doctor, "Please bring her around. It was so fast. One minute she was fine, the next she slumped over. Hurry, doctor, do something!"

"I'm afraid there is nothing I can do. This lady is dead."

"Dead! No! She can't be! That's impossible! She was perfectly fine only a few minutes ago. Please doctor, try again to bring her around."

"There is nothing I can do. I'm sorry. Did she have a heart ailment?"

"Yes, but she kept it to herself. I only found out about it the other day."

* * *

Man, what a relief! The funeral is over. Myra had a real nice send off. Lots of friends came. She would have liked that. Lucky for me, she didn't have time to change her will. I'm rich! Damn, I just committed the perfect murder. Time for me to get out of Dodge and commence living somewhere else.

"Josephine, come in here a minute."

"Yes, Mr. Allison?"

"Did you go by the Pet Palace and pick up Jezebel?"

"Yes, sir."

"Thank you. I bet that cross-eyed little devil was glad to get home. You may go. That' s all for now."

I just love having a maid at my beck and call! Now I'm sorry I played a prank on Myra. I know she worried about where Jezebel was. That cat was the only imperfect thing she ever loved. I think that cat and Myra were soul mats. Hiding her was not a nice thing to do, but it makes me chuckle. Was that the doorbell?

"Who in the hell could be bothering me? I'm in mourning up to my wazoo. Josephine, go see who's at the door."

"Mr. Allison, there are some policemen at the door who want to talk with you."

"Cops! Did they say what about?"

"Sorry to barge in, Mr. Allison." He didn't sound a bit sorry. "Could we speak to you in private?"

"Sure. That's all, Josephine."

"Mr. Allison, I'm placing you under arrest for the attempted murder of your wife, Myra Allison. Anything you say can and will be used against you in a court of law. If you cannot afford an attorney, one will be appointed for you."

"Now, wait just a damn minute. Just stop right there! My wife died of a heart attack."

"There was an autopsy."

"You can't do that without my permission."

"Sure we can and did. By law, an autopsy is required for any sudden death occurring under unusual circumstances. We found an undissolved capsule of Veronal in her throat, with your DNA on it from your saliva. Witnesses said you must have inserted it into her mouth from your mouth when you were pretending to kiss her. We tested the saliva from a whiskey glass you used. It showed the same DNA."

"But the doctor said she died of a heart attack!"

"Yes. She did die of a heart attack. Her doctor said she had been waiting for a donor to have a heart transplant. We checked all the local pharmacies about the Veronal and your former 'friend' admitted you conned her out of a capsule. And even better than that, there was a perfect fingerprint of yours on the capsule itself. You are busted, scumbag. You won't have a chance to enjoy the money you tried to kill her for, cause you'll be sitting in prison for the next twenty years."

I can't believe this is happening to me!

"Cuff him. Get him outta here!"

~

M. E. Cooper's experience in writing true crime gives her a solid background in writing realistic characters on the police force and realistic plots. You won't find her cozy characters discovering an obvious clue overlooked by professional detectives. M. E. is a relentless writer whose volume of work inspires all her writing friends. Her family's background as locksmiths, bicyclists and motorcyclists crops up in a large percentage of her stories. She is Mom to Guy Cooper, famous motocross racer, and grandma to Kenny Bartram, famous Xtreme Sports Cyclist.

~

Keyless & Clueless

by M. E. Cooper

Dave took the call on the mobile phone in his locksmith van and heard the panicky voice of a young woman. "I went out to walk my dog and I've locked myself out of my house! I'm not even dressed! Well, I mean I'm not naked, but all I've got on is my nightie and my house shoes. This is *so* embarrassing. How fast can you get here?"

He took down the address, consulted a map of the city, and tried to sound reassuring. "Ma'am I'll be there within fifteen minutes, sooner if I don't hit too many red lights."

Dave was driving while speaking into the phone. "You just sit tight and I'll get you back in your house in no time. I'm driving a white van with big blue key signs on the front and sides. It would help if you were watching for me, so I don't have to go door to door at the neighbors looking for you."

In a calmer voice, she said, "I'll be waiting on the curb."

With practiced ease, he swung the van through the city streets, thankful that traffic wasn't too heavy at 11:30 p.m. on a weekday night. Some guys didn't like to work evenings, but Dave didn't mind. The extra amount charged for after hours work just added to his savings. He could almost see the Stihl chainsaw he coveted. That baby could saw through tree limbs in nothing flat, and since he'd bought an acreage to clear for an eventual home site, making extra money was great.

He wheeled into the pricey neighborhood, noting that the houses each sat on a large lawn, probably an acre or two each. Then he caught sight of a curvaceous blonde, who admirably filled out a frilly T-shirt. The hem just reached to her fingertips. He swallowed a whistle. Wow! She was a looker. He didn't know whether he hoped she raised her arm to wave at him or not, as he was already sweating.

She held a dog leash in her hand, and a blonde cocker spaniel followed her mincing steps to the van window. That's when he looked down the length of her tanned, long legs, to see fluffy trimmed high-heeled slippers.

"Oh, thank you for coming so quickly."

"Nice dog!" Evidently that was the right thing to say, because the gorgeous blonde gave him a one thousand watt smile.

He bent over, letting the dog smell his hand before petting her ears.

"Her name is Daisy and I'm Debbie and I really appreciate your rescuing me! I feel like such a dummy! You know what they always say about blondes, but I don't think it's fair, do you? I have brunette friends who make as many mistakes as I do. And can you wait until I get inside to pay you? Because I don't have any money on me at all."

She held the ruffle of the shirttail out, as if to demonstrate that there was nothing on under it, and Dave felt his face blush.

He found himself grinning at her foolishly. "Let me take a look at your front door lock. You're welcome to sit in the van until I get the door open."

"Oh, you're so kind!"

Dave took his toolbox up to the door, wondering if she was the lady of the house or possibly a daughter. The Schlage lock presented no particular challenge, and within minutes he had it open. He didn't waste time looking at the entry way, only making sure to turn the knob on the inside to the unlocked position before closing it and walking back to the van.

"That'll be $25, ma'am," he told her.

She nodded at him, giving him a brilliant smile, then rushed inside, returning quickly with a $50 bill. "Keep the change, Dave."

"Well, thank *you*." He thought she must have gotten his name off his shirt, because he hadn't introduced himself. When she handed him the money, he had noticed neither hand wore a wedding ring. Maybe she was interested in him? He thought of asking her if she would go out for dinner with him sometime, but then reality set in. A gorgeous gal from this ritzy neighborhood wasn't going to go out with a locksmith who lived in a doublewide.

Dave smiled at her, feeling wistful, and remarked, "You've sure got a cute dog there. She almost looks like she's smiling."

"Daisy's part terrier. She has some crooked teeth that give her mouth that expression." Debbie wrinkled her nose, "I don't care if she's not a show dog; I love her anyway."

"Well, I guess I better be going."

"Did you have to go to college to learn about locks?" Debbie asked.

"No, although computer and math classes help. Mainly, I believe you either have a talent for mechanical things or you don't. My mom said I was always tryin' to take apart things from the time I was out of diapers. I just have this desire to understand what makes things work."

"I think that's wonderful." Debbie turned toward her front door.

"Maybe I'll see you again?"

"Maybe." She flashed that thousand-watt smile that made Dave's knees weak. She gave him a little finger wave of goodbye.

Backing his van out of the drive, Dave whistled a little tune under his breath. He'd tell the other guys at coffee about his interesting evening. And maybe he could find some excuse to be in the neighborhood some evening when she was out walking her dog.

But first thing in the morning, at their regular business meeting, he was given 56 apartment keys to change out, so the subject of the evening lock out call never came up. He had almost forgotten about it. That is, until he got a call from his boss. "There are two policemen here who want to talk to you, Dave."

"Yeah? You want me to finish this job or come back in now?"

"I think it better be now." There was a stern sound to his boss's voice that was not normally there.

What the hell? He didn't have a bunch of outstanding parking tickets. Not like some fellows he knew, who figured it was cheaper to pay the tickets than to lose time finding a space when they could be making money instead of driving around.

"This is Detective Whitten and I'm Detective Olsen. We'd like to ask you a few questions."

"Sure."

The two detectives might have been cousins, they were

so alike in appearance. Both were solid, thick-necked men with world weary eyes. The main difference Dave could see was that Whitten's ears jutted out from his head more than Olsen's. Neither man smiled or made any attempt to be pleasant.

Dave's boss said, "You can use that little room off the showroom for some privacy."

The detectives escorted him to the room, where Whitten said, "State your full name, address, and date of birth."

Olsen had a pen and notebook to write down Dave's answers.

After he'd given them the information, Dave said, "Look, I don't know what this is about. I don't have any parking tickets, and I got the title changed on the old VW junker I bought. Did the fellow who used to own it get a lot of tickets or something?"

"We ask the questions here. Dave Richards, did you drive a locksmith van, tag PY 7561, outside the residence at 1300 Graystone last night about midnight?"

"Oh, sure!" Dave felt himself relaxing. "Is it about Debbie, the blonde young lady who got locked out of her house? I let her in, she tipped me good and I got out of there. Why? Is something wrong?"

The detectives looked at each other for a moment, while Dave tried to figure out what their expressions meant. He couldn't read their silent communication at all.

"Let's start at the beginning. Tell us *exactly* what happened last night at 1300 Graystone."

Dave went over the call, repeating word for word, as well as he could remember, everything that was said and done. Still the detectives were not satisfied, and made him repeat it three more times.

Finally, his patience exhausted, Dave said, "What is this? Did that blonde claim I came on to her something? I sure didn't!"

Again, that silent look between the detectives. Finally, Whitten said, “Mr. Richards, no blonde lives at that address. An elderly gentleman, whose name is being withheld pending notification of next of kin, lived there alone. He was found dead, bludgeoned to death inside his home today, and a great deal of money and jewels are missing.”

“Wha-a-a-t?” Dave felt as if he’d been punched in the stomach. He knew his jaw dropped open but he couldn’t take it in. He shook his head, feeling woozy. It had to be some kind of mistake.

“A neighbor remembered seeing your van in the driveway.”

“I was there. I told you. But the only person I saw was the cute blonde. I didn’t see any old man or any robbery.” Dave shook his head, still finding it hard to take in.

“You didn’t ask this alleged gorgeous blonde for any identification?”

“Well, no. It was obviously her house. I mean, there she was in her little short nightie with her dog and why would she make up some story like that?”

Again that look between the detectives, but this time Dave saw a little pity in their glances.

“We know how the perp got into the house. The thief gained access to the house through you. We don’t know why the retired jeweler was killed. Maybe he came home at the wrong time, and interrupted the thief. Or maybe the thief didn’t want to take any chances of leaving a victim who could identify him or her. But you’re right in the middle of it.” Detective Whitten emphasized his point by poking Dave’s chest.

Dave’s temper flared, but he bit back an angry retort. He shook his head, thinking hard. “Hey, I’ll take a lie detector test. You can search my van, my house. I got nothing to hide. I’m not a thief.”

After some discussion, the detectives agreed it would be expedient to eliminate him as a suspect if he was innocent, so they could focus on the real perpetrator. They allowed him to drive his own vehicle to follow them down to the police department headquarters. Three hours later, which felt more like three days, he was finally told that he was cleared of suspicion and given permission to leave.

Back at work, all of his fellow workers wanted to know the details of his interrogation, until Dave felt sick and tired of the whole situation. He was glad when the boss told them all to get back to work.

That evening he got a call from a bartender at the Lucky Horseshoe Bar. "We got a customer locked her keys inside her car."

Dave got the address and turned his van toward the location. The bartender's voice had sounded sour, and Dave suspected the man had tried the old coat hanger trick and hadn't been able to open it.

Opening the door to the smoky dark interior, it took a moment for his eyes to adjust. Then he saw the bartender motion to a woman who was seated near the door.

A dark haired woman wearing big sunglasses and a bright Hawaiian print shapeless dress walked toward him. He wondered how she could even see with the dim light and dark glasses to boot, but decided it wasn't his worry.

"I'll show you where my car is parked."

Dave nodded and followed her as she led him outside and through the parked cars to the farthest edge of the lot away from the streetlight. He saw a dark Impala and was still unsuspecting until he saw the blonde cocker spaniel in the back seat.

"You!"

She pulled off the sunglasses so he could see her eyes, then reached up and placed a finger against her lips. "Shush. Please! I had to talk with you!"

"Yeah, you got some explaining to do. Did you kill the old guy?"

"No!" She looked at him with a wounded expression. "How could you think that of me?"

"Listen lady, I spent most of the day being questioned by the police about that murder-robbery. I'm not in the mood to play games with you. I'm calling the cops."

"Wait! You don't understand! I am just as shocked and appalled as you are about the murder. I had no idea. *No idea*!" She gripped his arm, "You've got to believe me."

"It's not me you've got to convince. You've got to convince the cops." He pried her fingers off his arm, gently but firmly. He was ready to walk back to his van and use the cell phone when she grabbed his arm again. This time her eyes widened with panic as she gazed behind him.

She gasped, "Savage! What are you doing here?"

Before Dave could turn or run he felt a cold steel barrel pressed against his neck.

"Don't move."

He hadn't heard anyone approach, but his heart sank. Either she was an Academy award winning actress or she was terrified of the person holding the weapon. Dave could feel his stomach tie up in knots and he hoped the other guy didn't sense he was near trembling. He tried to keep cool. "What's goin' on?"

She blinked rapidly and looked about to cry. "This is my boyfriend, Savage."

"Don't be tellin' him my name, you idiot!" The gunman reinforced his words by pressing the gun barrel deeper into Dave's neck.

"How did you find me?" she asked.

"You seemed a little too eager to see me leave, so I followed you."

"You lied to me last night! You told me it was your uncle's house. You said he owed you money. I thought you were just going to take what he owed you. I had no idea you were going to *kill* the old guy!"

"Shut up and get in the car. You drive, bitch. You," he pushed Dave's neck harder with the gun, "get in the back seat."

The dog was booted off the seat onto the floor with a yelp.

"Don't hurt Daisy!" she pleaded.

"Shut up."

Dave muttered under his breath, "You really know how to pick your boyfriends." A killer named Savage who kicked dogs around.

"What were you cookin' up with this fellow here?" Savage asked, and then answered his own question. "I'll bet I know. You were fixin' to get him to open the safe where I've got the loot stashed and beat it out of state, weren't you? I ought to kill you both right here!"

This was it! Dave thought he was going to be executed gangland style any moment.

Debbie began to cry harder, her shoulders shaking and her voice sobbing.

"Stop the bawling or I shoot the dog now!"

She sniffled but the loud sobbing ceased.

"Drive! And don't try any funny stuff to get attention from any cop cars."

Obediently, she turned the ignition key and carefully drove out of the tavern parking lot.

"Where to?" she asked.

Her boyfriend hesitated a moment before commanding, "OK, you want to get the loot. We'll go there."

She turned the next corner and drove through a bewildering number of streets. There were several times when he'd hoped the gun barrel pressure would lessen, especially when they went around corners, but Savage kept it pressed hard into his flesh. Dave knew there was a circular bruise on his neck from the weapon, but he didn't say a word. Anyone who could viciously bludgeon an elderly man to death would not hesitate to shoot an unarmed man.

Still disgruntled that the killer could slip up behind them before they knew he was around, Dave muttered, "Your dog is a fine watch dog. She didn't even bark when your boyfriend sneaked up."

"Why should she bark? She knows him."

Dave sighed. There didn't seem much to say. It worried him that the boyfriend didn't care that he had seen his face. That must mean he didn't expect Dave to be alive to identify him later.

They reached an abandoned building in a commercial warehouse area. Savage motioned both of them to proceed him into a hallway and then to a room which must have served as an office. Against one wall stood an immense Mosler Safe.

Dave understood immediately why the old fashioned safe had been left in the building. It was so extremely heavy, being the obsolete style with concrete reinforced doors and sides, that it was cheaper to abandon it than to have it moved. The large numbered dial had been damaged, but the Mosler had two nickel plated double levers and below that was a keyway slot. Dave thought it was remarkable that Savage had found a key to it.

As if reading his thoughts, the gunman said, "My old man used to work in this warehouse, unloading stuff." He bared his teeth. "Ain't I the lucky one to have a key to a big ole empty safe?" He held the key up and shook it at them. "I figured I'd leave it here for awhile, till I could arrange to sell it. Just in case anyone got curious, they wouldn't find any evidence on me. But my babe here got greedy, which was a big mistake. A big mistake."

"I wasn't going to turn you in," Debbie pleaded.

"Save your breath." Savage glared at them both.

"What are you planning to do now?" Debbie asked softly.

Again there was that evil smile. "Ain't you ever heard not to leave no witnesses?"

"Why don't you tie up the locksmith and leave him here? We'll be long gone by the time anyone finds him." Debbie was pleading for his life and Dave felt warmed by that.

Savage didn't bother to answer. While keeping the gun trained on them, he used one hand to open the safe and then began to unload it. He put the money and jewelry into a big soft-sided bag. Since he was forced to keep his eyes on them, he fumbled, dropping a necklace. When he saw what it was, he kicked it over toward her.

"Sorry, doll, you ain't goin' nowhere, either. The police are goin' to find that piece of jewelry by your body and there'll be a gun by good ole Davey's body. The police will assume a fallin' out of thieves. Of course they'll never find the rest of the stuff." He smiled then, with an evil expression that chilled Dave to his toes.

"You'll never get away with it." Dave said flatly.

"Yeah?" Savage's arm came up toward the woman.

Out of the corner of his eye, Dave saw the blonde cocker spaniel inching forward. How had she gotten out of the car? They must have left a window down.

"Goodbye sweetcheeks, it was fun." Sensing danger to her mistress the blonde cocker spaniel launched herself toward Savage. The dog bounded up and dug her teeth into his buttocks. Dave groaned, not in sympathy with Savage's pain, but in disappointment. The dog should have sunk her teeth into the arm holding the gun. Why hadn't the dog helped remove the danger? Then he realized, she was a *blond* cocker spaniel, not in the same league as a Lassie or even a rottweiler.

"Aarrgh!" Savage was screaming which led Dave to believe that Daisy had an even more tender part of his anatomy than his buttocks between her teeth.

"Call off your dog!" He screamed as he swung his arm around behind him, trying to dislodge the animal, firing the weapon blindly. Dave and Debbie both ducked as the shots went wild, ricocheting dangerously close to them. The feisty little spaniel hit the floor with a thud.

Dave lunged forward, landing a solid right fist to Savage's chin. The gunman was momentarily stunned and loosened his grip on the gun. Debbie screeched and flailed at him, causing the weapon to hit the floor. Dave hoped she had sense enough to grab it or kick it out of Savage's reach.

Dave hadn't been in a fist fight since he was a kid. He felt awkward and inept, but he knew Debbie's life and his own depended on his actions. He used his left fist in a hook, then punched him again with his right fist.

Savage was getting in some blows of his own. One landed square in the center of Dave's face. He saw crimson fireworks which felt as if they exploded in his nose. A red geyser drenched his shirt and mouth. From the corner of his eye he saw the dog recover and scramble toward Savage, where she gripped one of his ankles in her teeth. Savage screamed and Dave grinned at the criminal's pain and rage.

"I'll kill you. I'll kill you."

"I don't think so." Debbie's voice was calm and very cold. She held the gun with both hands pointed at Savage.

"Dollface, you wouldn't shoot me!" he blustered.

Debbie fired the weapon at his feet, causing him to jump backward and fall on his buttocks.

Dave heaved a sigh of relief, then tied up the criminal securely, using his belt and the dog leash. While he was making sure the bonds were tight, Savage cursed and yelled and tried to resist. Dave gave the leash an extra jerk for revenge. The curses and complaining continued.

"Shut up or I'll sic the dog on you again," Dave said heartlessly.

"Daisy, come here." Debbie's voice was calm.

"You can point that gun another direction now," Dave told her.

"I'm sorry, Dave, but you must sit down. Now! Take your shoes off. Tie the shoelaces together and toss them over to me."

"What?" Dave couldn't believe his ears.

"Do it!" Her finger pressed on the trigger and she fired a round at his feet.

He complied without another word.

"I saw this in a movie. It slowed down the pursuer."

Dave refrained from telling her he had seen the same movie. Taking a cowboy's boots from him in the middle of a desert with prickly cactus was different than taking the shoes of a fellow in a city with paved streets.

"Bye now." She edged around him to pick up the bag of loot, keeping the gun pointed at Dave.

The locksmith just shook his head. Even though she was acting criminally, she was still gorgeous. Her golden hair gleamed like satin, her incredibly blue eyes with their ridiculously long eyelashes reminded him of an Angel doll. He waited until she started the car before running silently up close enough to see the tag number. Then it was simply a matter of jogging through the deserted streets until he found a pay phone.

"I need to talk to Detective Whitten or Detective Olsen. It's urgent! About the robbery-homicide of the old jeweler. The killer is tied up in an abandoned warehouse and his accomplice is in a dark blue Impala, license plate number 34Y6K, probably heading toward the interstate. The loot from the crime is in the car."

He had to repeat himself, but he finally had the

dispatcher's full attention. Within moments, he was speaking with Detective Whitten, who turned away from the phone for a moment, ordering an all points bulletin for the vehicle Debbie was driving. Then he offered to send a patrol car to pick him up.

"That would be nice."

When the black and white unit rolled up, he grinned and got in. "I'm glad to see you. My locksmith van is at the Lucky Horseshoe bar and I need to swing by my house to get some shoes."

"OK, but first where is this warehouse and the perp? You say you tied him up?"

"I can direct you there."

Dave rather enjoyed seeing Savage's predicament, remembering that he was willing to kill in cold blood. The criminal snarled and cursed at the officers. "I need a doctor! I'm liable to die from these dog bites."

"Yeah, yeah. We'll take you in a minute." The first unit called for a second unit to take him to an E. R, after they shot pictures of the scene.

The officers took Dave to his van. Then he had to drive by his home to pick up some shoes. He noticed he was being followed by the patrol unit to the police station. They were taking no chances on losing a material witness, even though the detective had vouched for him.

Inside the police station he encountered a handcuffed Debbie in the hall.

He was surprised the police had apprehended her so swiftly, but then he realized that even in a city this size, there is not that much traffic at 2:00 in the morning.

Debbie looked at him reproachfully. "They say I'll be charged as an accessory to murder."

Dave just shook his head. She was so beautiful, her sad expression tugged at his heartstrings. He could not help feeling sorry for her. She hadn't tried to kill him, only delay him. “Maybe you’ll get a lenient judge.” His own words sounded falsely cheerful. He doubted that she would escape from being found guilty of conspiracy.

“I may be sent away for a long time.”

“Yes, I know.”

“They’re going to take my dog to the pound. I’m afraid they’ll put her to sleep. Will you take Daisy and keep her for me?”

Did he want another dog? Old Bingo was arthritic and nearly blind, but he would probably tolerate a young female. “OK.” When she seemed to be waiting for him to say something else, he added, “I’d be glad to give a home to the dog that came to my rescue. If it hadn’t been for Daisy, we’d both be dead.”

“I’m so sorry!” A solitary tear glistened on her cheek. “From the first time I saw you, I thought you were a good man, a kind man. I wish I’d met you first.” She looked at him, imploring him with her eyes, “Will you visit me and write me?”

He hesitated a moment. He’d never visited a prison before, but then he looked into her eyes. “Sure.”

“We need your statement, Mr. Richards,” an officer interrupted, breaking up the sad farewell.

“I’ll give you a statement, just as soon as I make sure my dog is not hauled off to animal control.” Dave walked briskly out to retrieve the animal.

Leaving the police station later that evening, he put his arm around Daisy, who was ensconced beside him. After all that had happened, he wondered if perhaps he was taking the best blonde home.

~

The Puppy's Bowl

1 cup peanut butter
1 stick margarine
1 12-ounce package chocolate chips
5 cups Crispix cereal
1 can mixed nuts
2 ½ cups powdered sugar

Melt chocolate chips, margarine and peanut butter on low heat. Place cereal in a large bowl and pour melted mixture over the cereal, stirring to coat. Add one can mixed nuts. Mix in powdered sugar. Spread on wax paper to cool.

For fun and lively comments, serve in a dog bowl.

* Serve humans only. Neither dogs nor cats should eat any chocolate.

~

Audrey Eggers writes fiction in several different genres as well as nonfiction and book reviews, but the mystery always draws her back. The puzzle to be solved, ordinary characters drawn into extraordinary circumstances and the expectation of justice served hold a fascination in reading and a challenge in writing.

~

Missing

by Audrey Eggers

From inside Henry Thompson's apartment Lucky barked loudly. Eugenia continued to bounce from one foot to the other while removing the key from the zippered pocket of her pink and orchid sweats. "Now, you quiet down, boy." She panted between words. "I need to keep moving. Can't cool down too fast."

Eugenia shook droplets of perspiration from her curly white hair. "It wouldn't be good for my old heart," she said as she closed her door.

After a shower and change of clothes she headed back out the door on her way to the Thursday Ladies' Luncheon. At the sound in the hall, Lucky barked again. Eugenia tapped at the door. "It's just me, Lucky. Hush up, now, before the neighbors complain."

After lunch Eugenia went shopping in Council Bluffs

with Corrie and Hazel. They stopped for tea and sandwiches and returned home after dark. Eugenia heard Lucky's whines as soon as she stepped off the elevator.

"Poor Lucky. Is Henry busy today?" She tapped at the door again and soothed Lucky. "He'll be home soon. Now you be a good boy while you're waiting."

On Friday she opened her door to Henry's daughter.

"Anita! What a pleasant surprise. Come in."

"I really just wanted to ask you about Dad."

"Henry? What about him?"

Anita gestured across the hall. "He doesn't answer the bell and Lucky keeps whining and barking. Do you have a key to Dad's apartment?"

Lucky scratched at the door, barked sharply and returned to his keening whine.

Eugenia was alarmed and realized she may have ignored Lucky's distress for too long. "Yes, I have a key for emergencies. I'll let you in."

As soon as the door opened, Lucky pawed at their feet, pushed his cold nose to their legs, and tail tucked, he circled toward the kitchen and back again. Eugenia's imagination took off. "This isn't like Lucky at all. Should we look around?"

"Lucky certainly seems to want us in the kitchen," Anita said. "Let's check that out first."

The dog's water bowl was empty. The food bowl was licked clean. And one cabinet door was scratched beyond repair.

Eugenia automatically reached for the magnetic child-lock key on the refrigerator. "His food's in that cabinet. Henry has asked me to feed him a few times while he was out of town for a weekend."

Eugenia left Anita to feed Lucky and slipped in to check the bedroom and bath. If Henry was injured – or worse – it was better that his daughter not be the one to find him. But there was no sign of Henry.

"Anita, do you suppose your dad had an out-of-town meeting and I forgot?"

"I don't think we would both have forgotten."

Eugenia didn't say, but her greatest fear was that her mind would fail and she could no longer be self sufficient. But her relief couldn't outweigh her concern for her neighbor.

"I'm going to see what's missing besides Dad." Anita marched into the bedroom and scrambled through drawers and closets, returned to rummage through desk drawers, opened and closed the refrigerator door, checked the bathroom medicine cabinet and then finally collapsed onto the sofa. Eugenia sat beside her and patted her arm.

"Now, dear, don't jump to conclusions. Let's think this through."

Anita jumped up and practically ran to the coat closet. "His hat, coat and briefcase aren't here. He left home on business." She pulled out a thick parka. "Even if he'd just gone to play cards at Senior Citizen's he would have this. He hates to wear his business clothes when he's relaxing."

Eugenia knew that Anita was ignoring the possibility of a lady friend, but didn't feel it was her place to say that.

Lucky returned to the living room and curled up on Eugenia's feet. She leaned over to pat and comfort him. His eyebrows came together in worry. His sad brown eyes looked up to his friend for answers.

Eugenia jumped to her feet. Startled, Lucky scrambled out of her way and watched. "Call his office and talk to the other agents. Henry may even be there. Lucky could be sick and needing a vet, and we may have been reading every thing completely wrong."

Anita rushed to the phone, but she stood there with her hand resting over the push buttons. "I just can't. If they don't know…."

She didn't finish, but Eugenia could interpret. One more piece of bad news would crush Anita.

"Would you like for me to go to the office with you?" Eugenia could ask the questions Anita was afraid to voice.

Only one agent and a receptionist were present at Welcome Home Realty. All the others were out showing houses, taking care of business.

"We pretty much work independently of each other. Coming and going, it's not that unusual to miss seeing another agent for several days at a stretch," said Rena Clark. "I can't be sure which day I last saw him. I think it could have been last week."

The receptionist was more helpful. "Monday afternoon." She paged through a spiral bound notebook. "I keep this for my own use. It's not required, but I've found it helps me to be more efficient." She put her finger on a line. "He was in and out several times that day and left the last time around 4:30."

She gave Anita an encouraging smile. "When the Smiths brought in the extra keys and warranty papers, I offered to call Lawrence Chance for him." She threw out a bit of insider's gossip. "You know he's really that famous mystery writer, Chance Lorenze." She waited for their response, so Eugenia smiled and nodded to nudge her on.

"It was the last warm day we had before the big snow came in. He said he would enjoy the drive."

"Did he leave then?" asked Anita.

"No. He took his mail into his office and made a few calls. When he came back out he was in a hurry. He mentioned he was taking a few days off. We didn't expect much business during the blizzard that was forecast."

Heavy snow had fallen Saturday night and Sunday with high winds blowing road-closing drifts for another day. The snowplows opened the main arteries by Tuesday afternoon. Wednesday life had gone back to normal – normal for northwest Iowa.

"I was in Cincinnati," said Anita, "and couldn't get back." She turned to Eugenia. "That storm. Do you think?"

Eugenia patted her arm and made soothing noises. "Maybe it's time we speak to the police. They can trace all kinds of information."

Anita's face creased with worry. She opened her mouth but didn't speak.

"Come on," Eugenia said. "I'll go with you."

Police Detective Patrick Carroll straightened folders and drew stick figures in the corner of his blotter as Anita put her face in her hands and wept. She fumbled in her purse for a tissue, and then gratefully snatched a handful from the box he offered. She wiped her eyes, blew her nose and apologized for losing control.

"Don't worry about it. You've given me the information I need to get started. Given his age…."

Eugenia sniffed her disapproval.

Detective Carroll shrugged and continued. "Anyone over sixty doesn't show up where he's expected, we look into it. That's what you want, isn't it?"

Eugenia shifted in her seat and let her expression tell him he just might have been able to explain himself this time, but for future reference he should be more careful.

Detective Carroll and Anita exchanged business cards and gave one of each to her. She added them to those she had picked up at Welcome Home Realty.

Arriving home, Eugenia went directly to her desk and wrote a list of the people and places Anita had mentioned to Detective Carroll. The diner on Fifth and Locust, King's Market, Senior Citizens' and the Methodist church choir. Her Thursday Ladies could fill her in on the choir and

Senior Citizens'. She added his coworkers at Welcome Home Realty, Lawrence Chance, the Smiths and the manager of their apartment building. She tilted her head to one side and considered her options. *Tomorrow,* she decided. *When I go for my race walking, I'll stop in for cocoa at the diner. Then I'll pick up a box of raisins at the market.*

Her doorbell rang, and she pulled the rolltop down to conceal the untidy desktop. Detective Carroll was at the door.

"I thought you might be able to speak more openly out of Miss Thompson's hearing. May I come in?"

"Yes, Patrick, come right in." *How fortuitous,* she thought. Aloud she said, "I'll fix us a nice cup of tea."

Eugenia sat a plate of oatmeal raisin cookies on the tea cart along with her best china cups, poured boiling water into the teapot and wheeled her offering into the front room. "I'm afraid you caught me unprepared."

Detective Carroll looked over the china, homemade cookies and steaming pot. "If this is unprepared, I will certainly call next time just to see what you consider prepared."

She gave him a coy smile. If this young man underestimated the elderly, he was in for an awakening.

"I spoke with your apartment manager."

"Doubt you got anything useful out of him."

"You're right there. Personally, I think he's more interested in his newest girl friend than in paying attention to what goes on here. For my own purposes, I prefer a nosy manager that has no other interests in life than to keep track of his tenants' business."

"So you've come up here to see if I'm the nosy neighbor. I really do have a full life. Besides race walking every day, I have clubs, committees and a very large family."

"I understand you feed the dog if Mr. Thompson needs to leave town. That implies a certain level of friendship."

Eugenia conceded the point. "I suppose I do know a good bit about his habits. His hours aren't regular, being in real estate. He seems to be home most nights by nine if not before."

"Women?" His tone gave weight to the question.

"He doesn't have a special lady friend as far as I know. There has been an occasional guest for dinner."

Eugenia sipped her tea and gazed out the window. "I don't think he wants to take the risk again since his wife died. Once over a cup of tea, we talked about the loneliness after being married for so many years. He said he missed the smells of being married."

"The smells?"

"You know, I said the same thing. The same way you did. He said, being the wife, I might not realize what it felt like to open the door at night, tired, thinking you didn't want to do anything but sit down and kick off your shoes. And then to smell dinner cooking or being kept warm in the oven. He said home smelled like that and like furniture polish and clean sheets and his wife's shampoo."

"You two were never…."

"Hardly. Do you realize how much younger he is than I?"

Following Patrick to the door, Eugenia said, "One of the women works with him at the real estate office. Rena Clark came a couple of times."

Eugenia took a seat at the Kumback Diner's counter and waited for Beth to bring her cocoa. "I believe my neighbor Henry Thompson eats here pretty often. Do you know him?"

Beth leaned on the shelves of glassware. "A police officer was in here asking' if I'd seen him this week, especially during that storm."

"Did you?"

"I wasn't here much myself during the storm. I told him Henry eats here almost every day. He liks our homemade soup – especially minestrone. We talk about what Anita has been up to – she was a couple of years ahead of me in school. But he really doesn't talk much about his own self."

"When was the last time you saw him?"

"He's such a regular, it's hard to say." She giggled. "You know that cop? He even asked if we dated."

Eugenia hoped that wasn't the only vein Patrick was following. This girl *and* herself? Really.

Apparently the waitress misunderstood her disapproving expression. "No. We did not. I dropped a hint with the handsome detective that I liked my dates a little younger."

At King's Market, Eugenia talked over a nice pot roast and her neighbor Henry with the butcher. The cashier wasn't chatty and didn't think she knew Henry Thompson. "How old was he?" She brought the manager "up to speed" and asked if business had picked up just before the storm.

"Oh, you know. People come in, buy milk, eggs, bread and toilet paper."

"How about Henry?"

"I was so busy…."

When Eugenia returned home she heard a noise from Henry's apartment. She knocked, praying that Henry would answer the door. But Detective Carroll was there instead.

"I thought…."

"Sorry. We haven't located him. Judge Gardiner OK'd a look around." He held up some envelopes. "I've picked up his phone bills and those from his office. Maybe we can locate someone who can help us."

"When you get through here, why don't you come over for a bite of lunch?"

"Well, it wouldn't exactly be regulation."

"In a town this size, young man, you just have to learn to bend some of those rules, or you won't have any friends at all."

"You may be right, but I believe in following the rules."

"Am I a suspect?"

He laughed. "No, Mrs. Franklin. You're what we call a valuable source."

"Good. If you find out I had anything to do with poor Mr. Thompson's disappearance you just go right ahead and arrest me. I wouldn't expect you to go easy on me just because I fed you cookies and lunch."

He held up his hands in surrender. "Yes, ma'am. What's for lunch?"

Detective Carroll didn't give much away, but when he left Eugenia was pretty sure she needed to talk with the people at Welcome Home Realty. She spruced up and looked herself over in the mirror. She wouldn't lie about wanting to buy a house. But real estate agents were trained to treat everyone as a potential client. The suit, hat and sensible heels wouldn't hurt her case.

Eugenia began by looking over pictures posted on the bulletin board and thumbing through the *Lenexa Real Estate Guide*. That brought the agents flocking around her and offering cups of fresh hot coffee. Rena Clark looked at her like she was pretty sure they'd met. Eugenia figured men were more susceptible to that helpless grandma act, so she zeroed in on Dutch Ingram, Lenexa High's star quarterback a few decades earlier.

After looking through albums and describing her dream home – actually the one she'd raised her children in – Eugenia asked, "Are you the one who sold the Smith's house to that famous writer?"

"Lawrence Chance. No, Henry Thompson snagged that

commission. And he earned every penny dealing with that fellow. An odd duck if I ever knew one."

And Eugenia also knew sour grapes when she saw them.

"He didn't want neighbors. He didn't want the house to be visible from the road cause he didn't want visitors. And he didn't want more than one bedroom cause he didn't want anyone expecting to spend the night. And who did you ever know to move from Florida to Iowa in the middle of winter?"

"How did his wife feel about that?"

"Oh, he was a widower. That just about persuaded Henry to throw in the towel. Said the man seemed glad to be rid of his wife. Didn't want to talk about her. Didn't want her mentioned. Completely rejected Henry's condolences."

"Everyone's different."

"His comment? Said he'd be able to meet his deadlines."

Eugenia felt just a little guilty about taking so much of Mr. Ingram's time, but she believed her motives were pure. She stopped at the library to do some research on the Internet. And at home she placed a few calls to Florida. Her memory of a Today Show interview with Florida author Edna Buchanan supplied the remaining pieces of the puzzle.

The next morning she called Detective Carroll and asked him to stop by right away. She was just taking an apple pie from the oven when he rang the doorbell.

"Did you get me over here to ply me with tea and baked goods again?"

"No, you and I are taking this pie to Mr. Lawrence Chase. I'll explain on the way."

"If this is police business I'm not involving you."

"I don't think we can get the evidence any other way. It's more difficult to refuse admittance to an old lady with an apple pie, and we do need to get inside."

He sat in her favorite rocker and crossed his arms. "Convince me first. Then we go. Maybe."

It was a seven-mile drive past the city limits to the writer's house, the last three miles on gravel and then a dirt road. The private drive curved through a stand of green ash and pine that sheltered it from any traffic that might happen by on the county road. As they drove around the last curve, Eugenia was surprised at the sight of the house. It was much larger than she had expected.

"If I hadn't read the description in the *Lenexa Real Estate Guide* I would never dream there was only one bedroom."

"He uses the former master bedroom as his office."

"Of course. An office. And the two rooms and one bath upstairs were combined when the Smiths added a hot tub, sauna and steam room."

Patrick rang the doorbell twice without getting an answer before he knocked loudly on the heavy wooden door. Maybe the man was such a fanatic for seclusion that he had disconnected the doorbell.

Lawrence Chance was not a friendly host. "Detective Carroll, I specifically asked you to call if you felt the need to ask me any further questions."

"Mrs. Franklin prevailed upon me to bring her out."

"I wanted to welcome you to Lenexa with a homemade apple pie."

"Very kind of you, I'm sure. However – "

Eugenia stepped into the house before he could explicitly tell them to leave. "This pie was hot, but it's cooling rapidly."

Mr. Chance ushered Detective Carroll inside, as well, and hurried them through the cold hallway to his office.

Eugenia sniffed a revolting odor before he closed the office door.

Floor to ceiling windows and French doors looked out over a snow-covered lawn sloping down to a pond. The bare limbs of weeping willows drooped to the surface of the water, frozen now except for a small area stirred by a family of ducks.

When Mr. Chance eased himself into the desk chair and picked up his coffee cup, Patrick asked Eugenia if she wanted a cup. She declined. If the smell in the hall was not bad enough, the sight of dirty dishes in and around the small bar sink quenched any thirst she might have felt. She also noticed pillows and quilts on the sofa. It seemed that Lawrence Chase lived in only this section of his big beautiful home.

"Let's get on with it, Detective. You've taken quite enough of my time already."

"As you like. I've spoken with the police and your neighbors in Florida. They were surprised to hear you presented yourself as a widower."

"I am a widower."

"Perhaps now. But not on the date you first called and spoke with Henry Thompson."

Mr. Chance did not respond. He merely scowled.

"They were also surprised at the delay between Mr. Thompson's inquiry and mine."

Eugenia stood up. "While you men discuss the case, perhaps I could use your powder room?" She smiled. "I would love to see the master suite."

"I'm afraid that's not possible. I'm conserving fuel and only heating the downstairs."

"Mr. Chance, I'm a born Iowan. A chilly room will not be a new experience." *Although I'm afraid the odor of that room might very well be something I have never previously experienced*, she thought.

He jumped to his feet. "Can anyone in this town take no for an answer?"

She looked him in the eye. "Could Henry? He missed his wife terribly and couldn't let go of your cold-hearted enjoyment of widowhood."

Detective Carroll opened the French doors and called out to his forensic team. "Search the entire house, but be especially careful in searching the whirlpool, steam room and sauna. Pull out the drain traps and bag what's caught there for the state lab. Look for any traces of blood, or human tissue. We may have to wait until spring to find the car."

He gave Mr. Chance the Miranda warning. Then he asked, "It's a lot easier to let the swamp and alligators do your dirty work, isn't it? Using a sauna and steam room to duplicate the heat and humidity of south Florida really isn't satisfactory. And the fact that a body can skeletonize in eleven days…does not mean it will."

~

Eugenia Franklin's Oatmeal Raisin Cookies

1 cup brown sugar
1 cup white sugar
1 cup shortening
2 eggs
1 teaspoon vanilla

2 cups flour
1 teaspoon baking powder
1 teaspoon soda
2 cups quick cooking oats
1 cup chopped walnuts
1 cup raisins

In large bowl beat shortening, sugars, eggs and vanilla. Add flour, oats, baking powder and soda. Beat at low speed until well blended. Stir in raisins and walnuts. Drop by teaspoonfuls on greased cookie sheet. Bake at 350° for 12 to 15 minutes or until browned.

~

Deborah Bouziden is the author of *Yankee Surrender* and *The Journal Wheel*, which guides her readers to set down today's history for tomorrow. Her style of blending genealogy and old journals into a contemporary cozy gives readers a sense of present day influenced by past love and loss. Deborah also writes articles, columns, fiction and nonfiction, teaches creative writing and speaks at conferences across the country. She served as OWFI president 2000-2001 and is regional representative for the National Association of Women Writers.

~

The Grave Hunter

by Deborah Bouziden

Karen Perkins stood and walked to the office door as her new client pulled into the driveway. She had talked to Patti Williams Mercer several times on the phone over the past few months and Karen lost track of how many emails they exchanged. The Williams family had been researching their family history. They had located everyone except a great, great, great grandmother. After looking for three years and finding nothing about her, they decided to contact Karen. Patti told her someone at the Historical Society recommended her. Karen had helped numerous families through the years find lineage lines. After she tracked *her* family down, and having spent all the years learning how, she decided to start her own research business.

She watched as Patti pulled a large box out of her trunk and stepped around the *Grave Hunter* yard sign. When

Karen first hammered the sign into the ground, she was the topic of many neighborhood discussions. Her closest neighbors finally asked her about it. When she explained she was a genealogist and specialized in finding graves of lost loved ones, she became a neighborhood celebrity.

Since then, she thought about renting an office, but decided against it because she wanted the people who contacted her to feel comfortable when they came for her help. Besides with the money she saved, she was able to travel to locations for research when she needed to and more importantly pass the savings on to her clients.

"I didn't know what to bring," Patti said as she stepped passed Karen who held the screen door open, "so I brought everything."

"Better too much than not enough." Karen shoved a blue three ring binder and stack of yellowed newspapers to one side of her worktable making room for the box Patti lugged. "Set it here." Perspiration beaded the woman's upper lip as she maneuvered the box around a chair and deposited it with a thud on the table's corner.

"It's pretty heavy," Patti said wiping damp curls off her forehead as she took a step back, "but at least it's all in one place."

"Did you have any trouble with my directions?" Karen asked as she pulled a chair out for Patti and grabbed another for herself.

"No, at least *you* were easy to find."

"Like I've said before, everyone leaves a trail. Sometimes it just takes a little creative looking."

"They said you've traced your family line all the way back to Adam and Eve and helped over fifty others do the same?"

"Yes, but the search hasn't always been easy and it *has* taken time. For all those I've helped, there's at least that many more I've not been able to do anything for."

"I hope you can help us," Patti said lifting the lid off the box. "We don't know where else to look. As I said in my e-mail, Grandma Lizzie is the only person's grave we can't find. There's a lot of conflicting information about her and then nothing. It's as if she ceased to be."

"I've found that sometimes, there are secrets in families," Karen said grabbing a pencil from a can, "How will your family feel if some deep dark revelation is discovered?"

"Won't bother the ones of us who want to know. There are things we found out about our other relatives that my great-grandmother's family tried to hide, but everybody has skeletons. That's in the past. It's our heritage, and no matter what we find out, it's our right to know."

"Good," Karen said, "I also want you to know everything I find, good or bad, will be documented."

Karen tugged on a legal size notepad. Maximillan, her black and white Himalayan had taken up residence on her stack of writing tablets. "Get up Max." He opened one eye and looked at Karen as if to say, *I don't think so*. Grabbing a corner, she slid the pad slowly out from under the snoozing feline who didn't budge.

"He's beautiful," Patti said leaning forward to look around the box.

"I've had him for over ten years. Found him in a cemetery. Someone dumped a litter there." Karen ran her hand down the sleeping animal's back. He didn't move. "I gave the rest away, but Max liked to climb in *my* boxes. As you can see I have a few." She glanced around the room at the cardboard containers stacked in the room's corners and under her worktables. "So I kept him. He's good luck. He even helped me solve a case once."

"Cute name."

"Maximillian was the man's name on the gravestone where I found him."

"Really?"

Karen nodded and sat down.

"Maybe some of his luck will rub off for us."

Karen laughed. "Perhaps. I've found this job is like a big treasure hunt, and you *need* luck, so maybe it will. In the meantime, what information can you give me?"

Patti pulled the box off the table onto the floor between them and started sifting through the papers. "I find it amazing that one's entire lineage can fit into a box," Patti said as she sat down again. "Hundreds of years boil down to one 14 x 18 x 10 flimsy container of documents, faded letters, and old pictures."

"But those papers tell an amazing story." For ten years, Karen had heard the tales of loved ones seeking answers to their past. Not once had she ever been disinterested in them.

Patti took out a stapled stack of paper and flipped through the pages. "We know that her full name is Elizabeth Ann Thompson Brown. They sometimes called her Lizzie."

Karen scratched notes on the pad as Patti spoke.

"She was born on June 16, 1836 in North Carolina to Jack Thompson, no middle name and Mary Anne Greer. Jack was born in 1808 in Mississippi and Mary Anne was born in 1811 in North Carolina. Mary Anne was a socialite from an influential family, had land, money. I believe records show her brother was mayor of a Mississippi town. Jack's family was fairly well off as well. Owned a plantation. Don't know if that has any bearing on Elizabeth, but...."

"Never know," Karen interrupted, thinking about the times she had overlooked one small piece of information only to discover it was the piece that completed the puzzle. "Is that information in here?" She reached down to pick up a census report.

"Yes, it's all here." Patti leaned forward to look at the census Karen held. "That's the Texas 1860 Census where we found Jack and Mary Anne. They had a ranch just southwest of Dallas. Elizabeth, her husband, James, and their five children are also in this Census. Three of the children were from his previous marriage and then their two. The first wife had died."

Karen flipped to a second page.

"Down at the bottom."

Karen wrote the date, names, ages, sex, and other pertinent information on her pad. "Her husband's name was James David Brown?"

"Yes. He was born in 1828 in Arkansas and was a farmer. They married in 1855; she was 19."

"It looks like you have traced her parents," Karen said reviewing Five-Generation Charts.

"Yes, and we've located where they're buried, but this is where things get all messed up concerning Elizabeth." Patti took a notebook out of the box and began flipping through its contents. "In a page of Mary Anne's Bible, one of my great Aunt's has it," she paused flipping more pages. "I have a copy in here." She studied a sheet. "Here it is. See it says 'In June 1860, Mary Elizabeth dead.'"

"And you've checked burial records?"

Patti nodded. "We've looked everywhere. Everyone was living in Texas at the time, so we assumed she might be buried there. The Census says they were there in 1860 and most of the family plots are there, but no Elizabeth. We've also checked Arkansas, but nothing."

"Why Arkansas?"

"While keeping track of where Elizabeth's husband, James David Brown, went, we found him in an 1870 Census in Arkansas with a new wife, Charity Simpson, and four more children. According to records they were married in 1862.

“We thought since we couldn’t find Elizabeth in Texas, maybe after the Census, they left, went to Arkansas, and on the trip or shortly thereafter, she died.”

“Sounds logical, but you didn’t find anything?”

“Nothing, but then again.” Patti continued digging through the box and retrieved a letter tucked inside a sheet protector. She handed it to Karen. “My grandmother has the actual letter. It’s framed, hanging on the wall. Been passed down from my grandmother’s great grandmother, Rebecca Brown Nelsen. It’s a letter, at least, part of a letter. Been burned.

“The story goes that Rebecca was living with her Grandmother Mary Anne when the post arrived. Mary Anne threw the letter in the fire, but Rebecca pulled it out, burning her hands pretty badly. She later told her daughter ‘it’s the only piece of mother I ever had.’”

“Interesting,” Karen said studying the missive.

“Can’t read much of it, but we do know it was from Elizabeth. Here is where she signed her name.” Patti pointed to the bottom of the page. “She apologizes for shaming her parents and says she’s with Philippe and his sister, Angel, in New Orleans, but look at the date. The year is 1863. She was supposed to have died in 1860.”

“There wasn’t another *Lizzie* who may have written it?”

“No, no one even close.”

“And this Philippe and Angel?”

“No idea. Strange though that they seem to be the last people she was with, at least that we know about.”

Max jumped off the table and knocked the page from Karen’s hand. He began investigating the box as Karen bent to retrieve the paper. “You don’t need to get in there,” she said as he peered over the side waiting for the right moment to make his move.

“I almost forgot,” Patti said reaching out to pet Max on the head. “Not that this is important, but we think Lizzie must have liked cats."

"Why do you say that?"

"Only guessing, but if you turn that over you'll see a copy of the sketch that is on the back of the original letter. She drew someone holding a cat."

Karen turned the letter over. There was no way to tell who the person in the picture might have been because the fire had burned through that half of the page, but Karen believed it to be a woman by the hand resting on the cat's back. The feline stared back at Karen as if it knew it was being drawn and would some distant day be remembered. Even though the copy was not in color, Karen believed the cat to be black and white. A black circle ran around one of its eyes like a pirate's patch. A black band of fur ringed the animal's neck and to complete the necklace look, a small ebony circle placed off center blazed on its wide white chest.

"Interesting," Karen said flipping back and forth between the letter and the picture. "Gorgeous cat." Max took that as a sign it was okay for him to jump in the box. Over the side he went. Karen lifted him out and set him on her lap.

"But you see how confusing this letter is. If she died in 1860," Patti said, "how can she write a letter in 1863? *And* if we're not sure when she died, how are we ever going to find where she's buried?"

"It can be confusing, but we'll see if we can make sense of it and find out."

"To some people I know the fact that we're looking for one person seems unimportant and pretty stupid. But the fifteen of us who have been searching, *really* need to know."

"I am *one* person who understands," Karen said remembering how she became obsessed with finding her ancestors. There were days when she couldn't and wouldn't sleep because she found new leads and was intent on following them up. "I'll get started right away."

With Max's help, Karen spent five days, going through the box of material. She familiarized herself with where the Williams had looked and the solid information they found. She made her own charts and table, cataloging people with places, making a timeline, and double-checking birth records against death records and census reports. She also spent a lot of time thinking about the facts Patti had given her and worked up a plan of action. Karen called people she knew in several states and asked them to watch for any information she could use as they researched. Attaching a $250 finder's fee for facts they may stumble upon was an added bonus.

Over the next four months, Karen searched through all Civil War records available.

"At one time, there were rumors she was a prostitute who followed Lee's army and even that she was a spy," Patti had told her on one of their weekly check-in phone meetings.

Karen looked through census records of any county named on any birth certificate, marriage license, and any counties surrounding that county. Patti was right. It was as if Elizabeth Ann Thompson Brown vanished…except for that letter. She also didn't know what to think of the people Lizzie obviously was with in 1863, but whom no one knew.

"I'm going to New Orleans in the morning," Karen told Patti over the phone. She was going to search records and look through cemeteries for another client. She had notified all her working clients, saving Patti until last. "I'll be gone three weeks."

"Are you going to look for Philippe and Angel while you're there?"

"I've thought about asking questions," Karen said

holding the letter in her hand, "but don't get your hopes up. Without last names, it's like looking for a specific grain of sand on the beach.

"I will be checking parish records while there and if I find anything I assure you, I'll follow up."

Two weeks passed quickly in New Orleans, and Karen felt her trip had been successful. She had found the records she needed for the Ruth family, but wanted to get them a complete set of census records to show the immense influence they had in the area.

On the third day scanning microfiche at the Historical Society, two names caught her attention. *Philippe Champeau, Angelique Champeau.* She stared at the names until her eyesight began to blur.

I am in New Orleans with Philippe and his sister, Angel. Karen had read the line so many times she knew it word for word. "Angel, Angelique," Karen muttered as she magnified the page and information in the small columns to the right. "Philippe," Karen whispered, "40, head of household, artist. Angelique, 40, sister, homemaker. Stephen, 12, nephew, student."

"Miss," an attendant said interrupting her concentration, "we're closing now. You'll have to come back tomorrow."

"I need a copy of this. It's the 1870 Census, Jefferson County, page 76 B."

The attendant, standing over her shoulder, wrote the information on a small notepad. "You can pick up your copy at the front desk when you sign out."

Karen looked once more at the names and information to make sure she was seeing what she thought she was seeing. Quickly rewinding the microfiche, she tucked it inside its box and put it back in the proper file cabinet before making her way to the front.

She rushed back to her hotel room and grabbed the

phone book. Her purse still rested on her shoulder when she found a list of Champeau's in the white pages. It wasn't until her thirteenth call that she knew she found something significant.

"Philippe Champeau was my great, great, great uncle," the man on the other end of the line said. "You should come and visit our museum and gallery. We have some of his paintings. They said he was a genius and would have been known world-wide if he hadn't been murdered…or so the story goes."

Karen listened and carefully wrote down the directions to the museum.

"We open at 10 a.m. Ask for Albert. I'll be happy to show you around."

Karen's alarm started beeping just as she had fallen asleep. She had tossed and turned for hours, switching the light off and on, studying Lizzie's letter, then the Census copy. She had a lot of questions to ask Albert about Philippe and Angelique. She hoped he could answer them.

Finding the building easily, Karen pulled into the parking lot at 10:01 a.m. Albert was not hard to find either, as he was the greying, bent older gentleman unlocking the front door. Karen was the museum's first guest of the day. *He sounded younger on the phone*, Karen thought as she followed in his shuffled footsteps.

"Philippe was my great, great grandmother's older brother," Albert said as they headed down a long burgundy hallway lined with busts standing guard on pedestals in front of green plants and six-foot portraits. Albert stopped in front of a painting of a woman. She stood, her deep brown eyes gazing at something in the distance. Her white lace dress pooled at her feet and her dark hair flowed around her shoulders like a cape. "This is my great-great grandmother, Angelique Champeau. Family and friends called her…."

"Angel," Karen said before she could stop herself.

"Yes."

"She looks like an angel." Karen continued to study the painting as Albert moved further down the hall.

"They say she was an angel in every way. Always helping the less fortunate, giving guidance or sanctuary to a soul in need." He paused beneath another portrait. "This is Philippe."

A spark of indefinable emotion in his black eyes and the firm set of Philippe's jaw held Karen's attention. There was something lazily seductive in his look. He wore his hair longer than most men of the period and for this setting, the dark, straight tendrils framed his face. One corner of his mouth curved upward.

"They were twins, you know."

"No, I didn't," Karen said, glancing at Albert then back to the painting. Philippe held his head high with pride and his broad shoulders proved he wasn't afraid of physical labor.

"Almost killed her it did when he was murdered. She told him not to go."

"Go where?"

"Back to Texas."

Karen turned to the elder man. "What part of Texas?"

"Around Dallas I think. That's where it all started…and ended," Albert said as he turned and moved to another room. "You can read about it if you want. We have most of Angelique's diaries." He paused. "Why the interest in Texas?"

"Like I said last night, I'm looking for one of my client's great, great, great grandmothers." Karen reached into the bag slung over her shoulder, brought out the letter, and handed it to Albert. "Lizzie said she was with Philippe and Angel in New Orleans."

"I recall a Lizzie mentioned in the story my grandparents used to tell. I remember the name because for the longest time, I thought it was Lizzie Borden." The old man chuckled. "Any more to…." he paused as he turned the letter over and saw the picture on the back. "Amazing."

"She was quite talented, wasn't she? It looks so real."

Albert looked up at her and smiled. "I think there is something you should see." He continued to study the drawing as he led Karen down a small corridor into another room. "This is a room of what my grandmother called 'his personal paintings.' Experimental if you will, except this one." He stopped in front of a painting that had already caught Karen's attention. "He kept it in his bedroom."

"Patti," Karen whispered as she looked into the face so like her client's. Her facial features were wide and round, cheekbones high and the same sky blue color of eyes. As Karen studied the picture, the only difference she could see in the painting and her client was her period style clothing and her hair. Patti's hair was cut short and worn straight. The woman's hair in the picture was curled around her face and flowed in long ringlets down her shoulders. And the cat. He was black and white with marking like those in Elizabeth's sketch. Karen felt as if she had stepped through time.

"Miss Perkins," Albert brought Karen out of her reverie. She had heard Albert speaking, but was so drawn to the painting she didn't hear what he said.

"I'm sorry Albert. This painting looks so much like my client, she could have posed for it yesterday."

"I've heard that sometimes generations removed will have relatives that look like their ancestors."

"No, I don't think you understand." Karen took out a small camera. "May I?"

"Yes, please do."

"The painting is like a photograph of Patti." Karen

snapped several pictures before stuffing the camera back in her bag.

Albert chuckled. “So finally, after all these years, Elizabeth’s family comes after her.”

“Her family wants to know what happened to her. This is the first piece of a big puzzle they’ve been trying to put together for years.”

“What are your plans for today?”

“This.”

“Then perhaps you would like to read some of my great, great grandmother’s journals. We have volumes of her writings, letters sent between relatives and friends. Maybe you will find another piece to your puzzle.”

Albert retrieved a pair of plastic gloves for Karen and got her settled in the library. You’re free to read any of the volumes here. These are the household records.” He pointed to one section of bookcases. “These are some of Angelique’s mother’s and father’s journals.” He moved to another section. “And here are Angelique’s. I think this is the time period you want.

“Letters are located over there,” he pointed to a shelf of notebooks. “If I’m not mistaken, you may find some of Philippe’s journals over here.” He pulled out a volume, looked at it and handed it to Karen.

“How is it that you have so much material on your family? Most collections have burned or been lost.”

“My ancestors were always involved in the arts, one way or the other and they collected. Philippe and Angelique’s grandfather owned a printing house and bindery in France. From land to ships to paintings and books, the Champeau family has collected and kept it all.” Albert laughed. “I leave you now with our impressive history.

“If you need anything, I’m down the hall.”

Karen watched the old man shuffle away. She took out

her pen and paper and opening Philippe's book, began to read.

By the time Albert came and told her the museum was closing for the day, Karen knew her trip would need to be extended. For the next ten days, she read, made notes, cried, got angry, and read more. When she finally finished writing down all the information she gleaned from letters and journals, her notes filled nine legal pads. She needed to visit one more place before she headed home. Mississippi held the key to where Elizabeth Ann Thompson Brown was buried.

* * *

Karen finished typing the last page of her notes and began printing them out. Max walked across her keyboard trying to get her attention. Since her return home three days earlier, he had followed her everywhere, getting in the way of everything she did. "I've written a tragedy Max," she said taking the pages from the printer, punching holes in them and placing them in a notebook. "One even Shakespeare would have trouble imagining." She flipped to the photo of the painting. She had blown it up so Patti could see the details. Max walked over piles of mail and sat down next to the pages Karen studied. *Meow.* "Yes, it's sad," she said running her hand down the cat's back. It was time to call Patti.

Karen finished packing the information back in the box as Patti pulled into the driveway thirty minutes early. Max decided he would investigate the contents once more, but Karen slipped the lid on just as Patti knocked on the door.

"It's open."

Patti came in smiling. "I'm so glad you found her," she said. "I could hardly sleep all night."

"Yes, well, I hope what I'm getting ready to tell you doesn't give you more sleepless nights." Karen motioned for her to sit in a chair and she grabbed the notebook from her desk.

"As long as she wasn't a serial killer, I'm sure I can handle it."

Karen smiled and wondered if she was *so* affected by what happened to Elizabeth, how would her descendants react when they found she had been wronged.

She felt like the pallbearer to a funeral gone badly. The information could not be kept secret anymore. Finally, after 120 years, Lizzie's remarkable and tragic life story would be told.

Karen glanced at her notebook as she began to tell the story. "Elizabeth first met Philippe Champeau in La Reunion, Texas, in 1855. She had accompanied her husband, James David, to the new settlement where they were to sell her father's beef. Philippe was one of about 400 colonists who were followers of the French philosopher Marie Charles Fourier. They hoped to set up a utopian society, but after just a year, the members were in trouble. In May 1856, Texas experienced an unusual blizzard, which destroyed all the settlers' crops."

Patti was spellbound as Karen read her ancestor's history.

> Shortly thereafter, Philippe starts coming to James and Elizabeth's place to learn about farming. Philippe's views on life are different from how Elizabeth was raised. He believes women should be treated as equal, and in an entry in one of his journals he writes, "Lizzie is very bright. It is sad she is forced to toil away on a farm and I told her so. The world offers much more than dirt and work, work and dirt. Her face shines when she smiles and

even the stars cannot match the twinkle in her eyes."

Philippe falls in love with Lizzie and she falls in love with him. For two years, she ignores her feelings, keeping her distance from him and making him promise not to see her. Then one day, while she is in Dallas, they meet again. They talk about how much they miss each other, all the time she reminds him she's married, has children. Their meetings are noted and soon family, friends, and acquaintances begin to talk about the cast glances, the familiarity between the pair, and the time they spend together.

In a letter written to Angelique, Philippe writes, "we do not know how much longer we can stay in Texas. I have told Lizzie I should leave, and then she could forget about me. She says she will die if I go. What am I to do? I love her so desperately as she says she loves me. Would you mind if she came with me to New Orleans? She is so dear, I'm sure you would come to love her as much as I do."

Three months later, Angelique writes in her journal that Philippe and Elizabeth arrive in New Orleans. "Lizzie is saddened by all the turmoil caused before they left Texas. She told me she dared not stay. Philippe would not leave without her. He had seen the cruel way her family treated her and he feared for her. She feared her husband would kill Philippe as he threatened if Philippe stayed."

Winter of 1863 arrives and passes. Angelique notes in her journal, "Lizzie has sent letters to inquire about her brothers. She is worried they are caught up in this hideous war. Any day we expect Philippe to rush off and do his duty. Such a silly idea. Since when does a Frenchman consider it his duty to die? He says he is part of this country and will fight with his countrymen. Lizzie and I have forbid him to go. She still has no word from her family. Philippe gave her a kitten for her birthday. She calls him Napoleon. I do not know which one she fawns over more, Philippe or Napoleon. She is a sweet soul. I wonder if her love for Philippe is worth losing her family and children. Sometimes, at night, I hear her crying in the garden."

Later that year, Philippe leaves to record the "horrors of war." Five months later, Lizzie becomes lonely and decides to join him. She writes a letter to her parents, telling them she is going to Mississippi and she will be looking up her uncle. Angelique journals that Lizzie has written her family at least once a week over the last four or five years. Only once did she receive a reply. It was informing her, James David had gotten the local priest to annul their marriage on the grounds of adultery, that he was remarried, and would be living in Arkansas. We don't know why Lizzie and Philippe didn't marry. Perhaps with his open philosophy, they didn't think it necessary.

Before Lizzie leaves New Orleans, she promises to write Angelique and let her know how she and Philippe are doing. When a letter arrives and Philippe makes no mention of Lizzie's surprise, Angelique writes her brother immediately. This begins Philippe's search and his "descent into madness." "My poor brother has spent the better part of this year looking for his beloved Lizzie," Angelique writes. "He stares at her portrait and Napoleon and mutters he never should have gone. He has tried to retrace her steps numerous times, but always comes home more discouraged than when he left."

Philippe and Angelique's spirits are lifted when a letter finally arrives from Elizabeth. Puzzled by where it is from and what it says, Philippe sets off immediately for Mississippi where Elizabeth says she is being held. Angelique writes, "We have heard from Lizzie, but do not understand it. She said she is being confined to a hospital and if we receive the letter, it is because the nurse she paid off has had pity on her soul and mailed it to you. She begs Philippe to come and rescue her. He left the moment he finished reading the missive. I hope to see our Lizzie soon and have her safely with us."

According to Angelique and Philippe's journals, Philippe is not allowed to see Elizabeth. Her family has had her committed and she is not allowed visitors. He tries again and again to see her, writing letters, contacting officials, but can get no help, no matter how much money he pays. He does find out from a nurse that Lizzie had a baby. It was taken from her and within a few months, the baby died.

From hospital records, Philippe is the only recorded visitor. It doesn't look like her parents ever tried to come and see her. Finally, Philippe decides to confront Lizzie's parents, so he travels to Texas. He arrives at a bad time. James David has taken Elizabeth's children to visit Jack and Mary Anne and is there when Philippe rides into town. There is an altercation and James shoots Philippe mortally wounding him.

"My dearest brother is dead," Angelique writes in her journal. "He should have never gone to that evil and barren wasteland."

It's almost eight years before Angelique hears from the Brown family. Elizabeth's daughter writes

> that she heard her mother died of pneumonia over the winter. "Grandmother will not tell me where mother is. I would like to visit her grave. Can you help me?"
>
> "I wrote the child and told her Elizabeth was being confined at Mississippi's North Regional Hospital," Angelique wrote. "Wish I had the strength to tell her how her grandparents kept her mother there against her will, how they paid to keep others out, and how they never once visited our sweet Elizabeth. Her family did not care to see the joy, life, and love between Lizzie and my brother. All they saw was the embarrassment they suffered because their daughter decided to go against society's morals and love another. Is there shame in true love? No, I believe not. I will not stoop to their level as I have laid my demons to rest. Let them sleep with their deeds and let their conscience deal with their secrets."

"According to hospital records," Karen said turning to the back of the notebook, "Elizabeth had only one visitor, Philippe, and he wasn't allowed to see her. There are several letters from Mary Anne Thompson requesting Elizabeth not be released if she is unrepentant of her ways and the promise of monies being sent to 'hold her.'"

Patti took a tissue from the box Karen offered.

"This page notes that, contrary to what her daughter was told, she didn't die of pneumonia, but she hung herself. She was buried in a grave outside the home as no one attended the funeral or claimed the body. The year was 1874. Her grave was marked with the year and her patient number."

"Will the state allow us to move her? If nothing else I'd like to put a headstone...."

Karen shook her head. "There's no way for you to do that now." Karen flipped to another page. "Around the turn of the century, the property where the graves were located was sold. The bodies were exhumed and buried in a mass grave. A single granite marker stands over the location today stating that 'here lie the patients of North Regional' and gives the dates 1865 to 1890."

"She wasn't crazy?" Patti asked studying the copied hospital records for herself.

"I don't think so." Karen leaned back in her chair and crossed her arms. "There is a lot we don't know, but from what I've pieced together, I think she was put away, hidden, punished because she embarrassed the family.

"I've encapsulated the story for you. When you've read all the notes I've written, you might want to take a trip to New Orleans, go through the Champeau Museum, read the journals yourself, and come to your own conclusions. Perhaps you and the others may want to go to Mississippi. The addresses of all the locations I visited are listed in the back." Karen turned to a page in the back of the notebook.

"I'll talk to them about it," Patti said. "It's a lot to digest."

Karen helped Patti out to the car with her box and the notebook of new information. "I think it's important to remember not how Elizabeth died or that she was betrayed by her family," Karen said, "but how she lived and loved. Her story should be a reminder that we all make our mark on this world and leave something behind, no matter what we do, haven't done, how we are treated by others, or what happens to us. Elizabeth left an indelible mark."

As Patti backed out of her drive, Karen thought about another of her clients. She didn't like telling sad and depressing stories to the families who came to her, but over the years she learned it was a necessity. Hearing her phone ring, she took the steps two at a time. Rushing inside, she picked up Max and grabbed the receiver. "You've reached the Grave Hunter. Karen Perkins speaking. Who can I find for you?"

~

Tombstone for My Pet

by Audrey Eggers

"What an interesting little tombstone. Is it really a grave?" She twirled a strand of hair around her finger and looked up at him through dark lashes.

"Yeah. Kelly's"

"Who was Kelly?"

"Kelly was my pet."

She gave him a fake slap on the arm. "I figured that, Silly. Was Kelly a dog?"

He shook his head no. His smile showed his enjoyment of their little game.

"A cat?"

He hooked an arm around her waist and pulled her close. "No. I really don't like to talk about it. You're ruining the mood."

"I'm sorry. I shouldn't ask so many questions."

"Let's sit on the porch swing and have a glass of wine."

"Ooo. So romantic." She batted those long lashes.

He nuzzled her neck and placed a soft kiss behind her ear. "Oh, Honey, your hair smells so sweet."

She pulled away just a little. "I bet you call all the girls 'Honey.'"

"How about Sweetie?"

"Sounds like candy."

"Come here, My Pet. Stop acting so coy."

~

Judith Sexton has a mind full of stories and beautiful ways to tell them. Give her a subject, style and word count and she produces a tale to relish. Her assignment in this case: Give us another mystery short story, twelve to fifteen pages long, no less than 3700 words, and add a pet or curl a cat up in someone's lap. She is an editor's delight. Readers will most likely agree that she is a mystery lover's delight as well.

~

A Greater Trespass

by Judith Sexton

Detective Sergeant John Larrimore gazed down the street where his grandparents lived during his boyhood. The budding trees allowed a clear view of the houses on either side. The character of the street had changed. Many of the original Victorian houses remained, their cupolas and fanciful gingerbread in varying states of repair. A few had been converted to apartments, others replaced by boxy modern duplexes. Generations of old oaks and elms had been destroyed to make room for the new buildings. This end of the street, furthest from the busy cross street, was less changed, although he was sure most of the old neighbors were gone. His grandparents' old home, directly across from the murder house, looked much as he remembered it. The house beside it had cars parked in the driveway and on the front lawn. Bicycles were attached to the wall, and a hammock hung from the porch ceiling. He surmised college kids lived there.

The house where the victim was found showed signs of neglect, its paint faded and the large lot overgrown. The place had once belonged to the Harris family, but that was years ago. Now it stood empty. Miss Florence Penn's house, on the left looked just as he remembered it. The maple in front and the willow in the side yard were much larger; thirty years was a span of time for trees as well as boys.

Wondering if Miss Penn still lived in her old home, he climbed the steps to the wide front porch, and rapped with the worn brass lion's head knocker. His partner joined him as he waited at the door.

The frail old woman who answered the door leaned heavily on a silver-knobbed cane. Her once dark hair was silver, but still worn in a coronet of braids on her proudly held head. And instead of a dark housedress, she wore a soft fleece top and pants in dark blue.

"Miss Penn? You may not remember me. I'm John Larrimore and this is detective Sherry Jensen."

"Johnny?" She leaned toward him, peering with old, old eyes. "Of course I remember you. You were the best paperboy I ever had. And you have the look of your grandfather. All that dark hair and brown eyes. He was a handsome man. But where are my manners! Keeping you and your friend at the door. Come in, both of you." She led the way to her parlor.

Behind Miss Penn's back, Sherry looked at John and raised her brows. "Johnny?" She mouthed silently.

He scowled at her. "Forget it!" he whispered.

"I suppose you're here about that – that man next door. What a terrible thing." She shook her head. "Nothing like that ever used to happen here in Athena. It's all these new people moving in."

The room felt overheated after the fresh April breeze. The central heat was on, and coals still glowed in the fireplace. "I hope you're not too warm in here," Miss Penn said. "My old bones get cold, and I haven't felt warm since I heard about Mr. Owens. He was a dreadful man, so pushy, but still…." She shivered and rubbed her arms.

"It is distressing," Sherry agreed.

"Would you like tea or coffee, and cookies?" She looked from one to the other.

"We're fine, Miss Penn. You don't need to go to any trouble for us."

"It's been so many years since I saw you, Johnny. I'm not going to let you go away without a little hospitality!" Leaning on her cane, she refused Sherry's offer to help and left the room.

The ticking of the grandfather clock in the entry was loud in the silence. There was a smell of old furniture polished with lemon and wax, and the fragrance of potpourri hovered like the ghosts of summer roses.

"This place is a museum," Sherry said. "I'll bet that's a genuine Aubusson carpet."

"This room hasn't changed since I was a kid. Miss Florence used to bring me in here when I came to collect for my paper route. She always gave me cookies then, too." He looked at the faded cabbage rose wallpaper, the small tables, the silver framed photographs of people in old-fashioned clothes, and the gleaming mahogany piano. "Those are probably even the same ferns."

Miss Penn came back into the room pushing a small teacart. John and Sherry both jumped to help her, but she waved them away. Sitting in a straight-backed chair, both of her small feet firmly on the floor, she poured steaming Earl Grey tea into bone china cups.

As John took his cup from her, he smelled the same sweet floral talcum that his grandmother had used. "I've always remembered your cookies, Miss Penn."

"I loved to bake," she said sadly. "But these are from the bakery – I'm not able to do much cooking now. My eyes, you know, and I tire so quickly."

He sipped his tea, the cup fragile in his big hand. "It's good to see you again. It's been a long time."

Miss Penn nodded. "It's hard to realize so much time has passed. I can hardly believe your grandparents have been gone for more than thirty years now." She offered more tea to Sherry, and went on, "If your grandfather had been here, the zoning would never have been changed. As it was, there was no one to stand up to Mr. Owens. And now he's bought up most of the houses, and cut down so many trees. He despoiled our street."

"How well did you know Macky Owens?" John reached for another shortbread cookie.

"Not well." She sipped from her cup and dabbed her lips with a linen napkin. "He came around wanting to buy my house, offering half of its worth. Did you know he planned to tear down the Harris place and build an apartment house? That's why he wanted my house and yard, so he could build more units."

"It's sad to see the old neighborhoods go," Sherry murmured. "Had Mr. Owens been here recently?"

Miss Penn's hand tremored as she placed her cup on the table beside her. "As a matter of fact, he stopped by just yesterday. Around suppertime. And I told him again that I wouldn't sell." She looked at John, her eyes wide. "You don't suppose – do you think he was out there all night?"

"I can't say for sure," he answered, "but it looked as if he had been dead for several hours."

"And the paper boy found him." She reached for her cup again. "It's a shame that poor child had to see him. I've always thought he was too young to have a route."

"Miss Penn, was Mr. Owens alone last night?" Sherry

asked gently. “Did he seem worried or upset?”

“I really wouldn’t know.” She looked as if she wanted to sniff. “He came to my door alone. I didn’t let him in, of course. He was such a vulgar person.”

John held back a smile. Miss Penn hadn’t changed in all the years since he had known her, except for the physical signs of age. “Do you know Robert Schwartz, in the house on the other side of the Harris place?”

Miss Penn nodded. “We’re acquainted. I see him when I’m out in the yard. And he came over here after Mr. Owens tried to buy his house. He was as upset as I was about Owen’s plans to build.”

“So you don’t know anything about his family, or friends?” asked Sherry.

She looked at Sherry, her brows lifted. “How would I?”

John asked the next question. “Did you hear anything unusual, at any time last night?”

Miss Penn shook her head. “My windows were closed. And of course, my hearing is not what it used to be.”

After thanking her for her time and having their offer to help with the tea things declined, John and Sherry left to canvass the neighborhood. As they walked toward the next driveway, Sherry looked back at the tall Victorian house.

“Miss Penn isn’t fluttery like most little bitty women.”

John raised his brows. “Little bitty? Do I detect sizeism?”

“Oh, you know what I mean. Most of them act sort of helpless, girlish, no matter how old they are. I’m always afraid I’m going to trip over them or something.”

“They’re probably intimidated by a Valkyrie like yourself,” he teased. “Afraid you’ll step on them.”

“Not funny. But you know what I mean. Miss Penn is so reserved and so dignified.”

“She’s always been like that, ever since I can remember. But my Granddad said she was a real hellion when she was a kid. He called her "Florrie" and said she tried to do everything he did – and usually bested him."

They found two other owners who had seen the victim the night before, but learned nothing from them. One of them did refer to Owens as a "bulldozer." They saved the house with cars on the lawn for last.

John knocked several times on the door before a muffled voice yelled, "Stop hammering and come in." The door was unlocked and John and Sherry walked into a darkened room strewn with inert bodies both male and female. They were met by an extremely homely animal which looked like the product of an illicit union between a bull dog and a poodle. The dog, who wore a bandana in school colors around his neck seemed to be hung over as well. Or very mellow.

"Shut the door, dude. Before Dude gets out." It was impossible to tell who had spoken.

John found the light switch and flipped it on. Muffled groans and complaints came from bodies sprawled on couches and the floor. "Time to wake up kids. The cops are here."

It took hours to sort the kids out and take statements that were fuzzy at best. There were full time residents (six guys) and those who had crashed there the night before (an additional five guys and six girls). Then they tried to determine who else had attended the Friday night beer bust. Which was a difficult matter, since people had come and gone, and the memories of none of those present agreed.

Back in John's office, the two detectives went over their notes.

"Nothing. No weapon, no noises, nobody saw nothing." John groused. "May have been a mugging – or somebody made it look like one by taking his wallet. Macky Owens was a real wheeler-dealer and made a lot of people unhappy with his zoning change. Then just to make things interesting, we've got at least two dozen kids near the scene, none of whom can accurately account for their own or each others' whereabouts. And if the murder weapon is in that house, we'll never be able uncover it."

"The kids seem like typical students, not the kind to bump somebody off."

"Hah! Don't you know that's the most likely kind? As in, 'he was such a nice young man. Just the boy next door.'"

"Sarge, you are so cynical. But I suppose one of them could have needed money for more beer and chips, and hit Owens harder than he intended."

"It's possible. Owens was flashy. Big car, fancy clothes. He looked like somebody who would be carrying a roll." John tapped his pencil on his desk. "If we knew what was used to bash his head in, we might have a better idea whether it was premeditated."

"That one kid, the big blond guy, Zach Beaumont," Sherry looked through her notes. "He seemed more antsy than the other kids."

John nodded. "I noticed him. His ID looked bogus. Close resemblance, but not quite. Like maybe it's his older brother's photo. I didn't have time to deal with underage drinking this morning. But I figure we'll end up talking to all those kids again, if nothing turns up."

Sherry leaned back in her chair. "I kind of like that neighbor – Schwartz. He's known to have a hot temper, he quarreled with Owens and he has a record for assault."

"A very old record. When he was much younger. And if his alibi pans out, we've got squat."

"What about your friend, Miss Florence?" Sherry teased. "She didn't like Macky Owens. He was vulgar."

"Poor old thing. She's the last of her family. My grandparents were the closest friends she had, and she never let them too near. I think Granddad was the only man she liked or trusted. And that was because they played together as kids." He put the pencil down, and leaned back in his chair.

"Once she called me at my grandparent's house, and scolded me for throwing her newspaper into her begonias or whatever. I said something about her being a crabby old maid, and Granddad about took my head off. He said she'd had a lot of pain in her life. First, her mother died when she was about ten or eleven, leaving a baby girl for her to take care of. She had to grow up real fast. Her father was a banker, an important man in the community, but he was very stern with her. Then he went to Chicago on a business trip, and nobody ever heard from him again. Miss Penn wasn't even twenty when he disappeared."

"What happened to the sister?"

"That's another sad story. She died of polio while she was still in high school. And Miss Florence has been alone ever since, as far as I know."

"Poor Miss Florence. She must have been a beautiful young woman. Maybe she had a tragic love affair. She may have loved a soldier who died in the war or something. She's the right age."

John grinned. "Been reading romances again, Corporal?"

"I get them the same place you buy your westerns. What is that series you read, "Long Iron, or Big Leg, or whatever?" Sherry retorted.

"It's Long Arm, as in the long arm of the law. The stories are fictionalized accounts of historic events. Very interesting plots." John put on a serious face.

"Right. And of course the hero had to take care of the ladies."

"Well, of course. It was a tough job, but a good law man is always prepared."

Sherry rolled her eyes. "I'm going to get a refill Do you

want any more coffee?"

John shook his head and picked up the phone. He was still talking to the coroner when she returned, his expression glum. When he finished, he turned to her. "Blunt trauma to the head. They found wood fibers – bark in the wound. So he was hit with a branch – stick of wood? Time of death between seven and ten yesterday evening. What time did Schwartz say he was bowling?"

Sherry flipped through her notes. "Says he got a burger at the bowling alley after he got off work, around five thirty. Then stayed until nearly midnight, tournament bowling. Should be easy enough to verify if he was there when he says."

"He was my favorite suspect. But that would have made life too easy. We're going to need some luck to solve this one." John rubbed his eyes. "The beer blast was in full swing down the street, people coming and going, in varying stages of shit-face. The chunk of wood could work in a crime of opportunity. But this just doesn't feel right for a random hit. His Mercedes was parked in the driveway all night, with the keys in it, and his briefcase and stuff. It doesn't appear to have been touched. Unless it was just the beer money thing. We've got a bunch of people to rule out."

He got to his feet and stretched. "Let's go back to the neighborhood. We'll look around, and talk to the kids again. Maybe we overlooked something, or we can shake something loose."

Sherry groaned. "At least they should be more awake by now. If that's any help."

The wind had picked up while they were in the office. Sherry pulled her fair hair back and fastened it into a low ponytail at the nape of her neck as John looked for a parking place.

The curb was still lined with cars on both sides of the

party house. John parked in Miss Penn's driveway. "I'm sure she won't mind, but I'll ask her real quick if we can park here."

As they got out of the car, Sherry pulled on her suede jacket. "It's getting colder instead of warmer."

A horn blasted in the street, and they turned to see what looked like a fuzzy pig strolling along in front of a pickup truck. The driver banged on his door and yelled an obscenity, then threw a soda can at Dude. The dog scuttled into Miss Penn's yard and under low growing branches of a large forsythia bush.

"Poor Dude." Sherry ran across the lawn and knelt in front of the shrub. "It's okay, sweetie. You can come out now."

"*Sweetie*?" John chuckled. "That dog would probably cuss you out if he could talk."

"He is a sweet little guy. It's not his fault he lives with a bunch of foul-mouthed kids." Sherry ducked her head to see under the branches. "John? There's a letter under here. I can't reach it."

He knelt beside her and stretched his arm under the bush. Dude gave a funny little growl and scooted to Sherry. She caught his collar under the bandana and held on to him.

John half crawled under the shrub and came out with a clean white envelope. "It's addressed to Macky Owens, and the return address is Wallace Abstract Company. It's empty, but it can't have been here more than a day."

Sherry brushed the knees of her pale blue jeans. "It's too much to hope that the letter is here too."

"I'll look around while you take the Dude home," John said.

After a quick survey of the other shrubs in the yard and around the foundation of the old house, they gave up on finding the letter. "Let's see if Howard Wallace can tell us more about what Owens was doing. We'll get back to the kids later."

"It's Saturday. " Sherry reminded him. "Will his office be open?"

"Probably not. But Wallace is my fishing buddy, so I can track him down."

Back in the car, John used his cell phone and soon was talking to the abstract office owner. Sherry listened as John explained what he needed to know. When the conversation ended, John sat back with both hands on the steering wheel.

"Well, Howard's opinion of Macky is about the same as everybody else we've talked to who knew him. This week Wallace and company surveyed the property where Owens was found. He also paid for them to survey Miss Penn's lot."

"And? You must be going somewhere with this."

"Patience, my child. It seems that the property line is off by about fourteen feet on Miss Penn's lot. To the advantage of Macky Owens. He was crowing to Howard that he was sure he could get the old lady to sell."

"Nice fellow. But do you think this has any bearing on his death?"

John shrugged. "It's worth checking out, anyway."

"You don't really think that poor old woman could have done it? Would the survey report have been enough motive for Miss Penn?"

John shrugged again. "I wouldn't think so. She still would have a large lot, almost double sized."

"Robert Schwartz wouldn't have been happy about any success Macky Owens had getting a bigger toehold in the neighborhood."

"Let's see what he told Miss Florence." John reached for the door handle. "Let me do the talking, okay?"

"Sure." Sherry followed him up the drive to the wide front steps.

Miss Penn opened the door almost as soon as John

finished knocking. “Johnny, Miss Martin. Come in please.” She led the way to the quiet parlor.

“Miss Florence, we need to ask you some more questions,” John began. “Did you know that Macky Owens had your lot surveyed?”

Sitting very straight in her armless chair, she nodded. “If you know about that, then you know what he found.”

“Your boundary line is off,” John said. “Did you know before the survey was done?”

“I never really thought about it,” she answered. “There was never a fence between the two yards. Papa always had the grass mowed that far over, and I just assumed that it was our property.”

“Were you upset when Owens told you about the report?”

“It wasn’t the size of the yard. He was going to cut down the willow tree, and start digging, whether I sold to him or not. I couldn’t let him do that.”

“Why not, Miss Florence,” John asked, his voice gentle.

“Because of Papa. Papa’s there, under the tree.” She looked down at her hands, twisting and twining her handkerchief.

“People said he went off on a business trip, and never came home.” John reminded her.

“I let everyone think that. I couldn’t tell anyone….” Her voice trailed away.

Sherry looked at John and lifted her brows. He nodded.

“Miss Florence, do you understand that I need to read you your rights?”

She nodded.

When he finished, John looked down at the small bowed figure. “Do you want to call your attorney? You can do that now if you want. It might be a good idea.”

“No” Her voice was almost a whisper. “Having him here wouldn’t make any difference. It’s been such a weight on my mind…my father…I hated him, but I couldn't tell anyone."

"Why did you hate him, Miss Florence? Had your father done something bad?"

Miss Penn turned almost eagerly to Sherry. "Yes," she whispered. "He – came to my bed not long after Mama died. He said it was my duty to take her place. She lowered her gaze again to her hands in her lap. "I knew it was wrong, but there wasn't anything I could do. He said if I told, nobody would believe me, and then he would send me away to a school for bad girls."

Sherry knelt by Miss Penn's feet and took her hands. "What happened to your father?"

Miss Penn gave a choked sob. "The night before he was to leave for Chicago, he – he went in Katherine's – my sister's room. He was going to – you know." She pulled her hands away and went back to shredding her handkerchief. "I couldn't let him do that. I hit him hard right at the back of his neck, with a vase. He couldn't move, couldn't breathe. He just kept staring at me until his eyes went dead."

Sherry put her arm around the older woman. "You poor thing. What did you do then?"

Miss Penn swallowed hard. "It was night, and raining. The rain had been coming down for days, so I knew the ground was soft. I put on some dark clothes, and went out in the yard. I dug and dug, all night long. It was almost daylight before I had the hole deep enough. Somehow, I got him out there, and covered up. And that morning I planted the willow over him."

All the time she was speaking, she kept picking and tearing at the white handkerchief. "And I knew when Mr. Owens started building over there he would find Papa's bones."

"Was that why you killed him?" John asked gently.

She nodded. "It was the only way I could stop him. He was laughing, showing me where the property line ran, right between the willow and the woodpile. He bent over to pick up something, and I picked up a piece of firewood and hit him as hard as I could."

John knew he would see those delicate age-spotted hands and tiny brittle fingers twisting and pulling at the square of cloth until the last day of his life. "And then you built a fire in your fireplace, and burned the wood, and Owen's wallet."

"That's right. If he hadn't been such a dreadful man, you know, I couldn't have hurt him."

"I know, Miss Florrie. I know." John touched her fragile shoulder. "Is there anyone you would like to call before we take you downtown?"

"No." She sighed. "No."

~

One last story from ***M. E. Cooper*** illustrates the range of her talent. She can't make everyone think logically or choose wisely, but her stories can illustrate the folly of abandoning logic and wisdom.

~

Just a bunch of Junk

by M. E. Cooper

Cathy looked at her friend Barbara and wondered when she'd become so cynical and bitter. She had been listening to a tirade which had gone on far too long. Trying to placate her, Cathy suggested, "Perhaps your former boyfriend's mother thought you'd really appreciate these things."

"Appreciate junk!" Barbara's voice rose two octaves. "She betrayed me! Just like that lousy son of hers, when he asked for his engagement ring back. Hazel always promised me that when she died she'd leave me a nice little nest egg, and what do I get?" Pointing to a stack of items, she shrieked, "Junk! Nothing but junk!"

"But she did leave her darling cat," Cathy reminded her, petting the Persian cat who twined about her legs.

At that moment the doorbell rang. Cathy was relieved

as Barbara went to answer it. She sneaked a peek at her watch, deciding as soon as she could, she'd leave Barbara to stew by herself. Frankly, she was tired of hearing her complaints.

"Mr. Atwood is here from the auction company. I called him before I saw what miserable stuff Hazel left me."

Cathy nodded to the distinguished looking gentleman. She recalled that his auction company had a prestigious reputation.

Barbara continued with her litany of complaints. "I wouldn't have bothered you if I'd actually looked at the stuff first. Of course, I won't expect you to appraise this junk."

He looked at several of the items and raised his eyebrows. "You want me to sell this for you on consignment?"

"Oh, no." Barbara gave a sour laugh. "Just give me a hundred dollar bill and you can haul it all off."

"Just a minute, Barbs," Cathy protested. "I've heard some old fountain pens are worth a lot of money."

"These don't even work!" Barbara complained. "Look at this: a bowl so ugly I wouldn't use it for the cat's dish. A bunch of old letters and this monstrosity of a picture frame. I never liked the old biddy, I just sucked up to her because I thought she was rich."

Cathy was shocked that Barbara would be so blunt before a perfect stranger.

Mr. Atwood said carefully, "Are you positive that you don't wish an appraisal?"

She shouted, "I don't want this junk!"

"Very well, I'd like you to write down on this paper that you are declining my appraisal and selling it to me for.... What did you say? Was that one hundred dollars?"

Cathy looked back and forth between Mr. Atwood and

her friend. She sensed something was amiss from his calm expression but the anger on Barbara's face as she hastily dashed off the words made her hold her tongue.

He asked Cathy to sign it as a witness. After the door closed behind the man and his armload of possessions, Cathy sighed. "I hope you don't regret that."

"The only thing I regret is ever being nice to that mealy mouthed woman who lied to me just like her son did."

Cathy left then, feeling sad that Barbara was so full of animosity.

It was a month later when Barbara called Cathy. "I saw an Atwood's auction flyer. I'll come by and pick you up. I want to see what fool would buy that junk."

The first item they both recognized was the hideous bowl. Holding it aloft the auctioneer said, "This is a fine example of 14th century Japanese pottery. What am I bid for this tea ceremony bowl?" The bidders were mostly from museums. Cathy and Barbara looked at each other in shock as the price went over $150,000.

"And I thought it was too ugly for a cat's dish," Barbara whispered.

"Next, we have some letters from William McKinley to Theodore Roosevelt. And a few signed by William Jennings Bryan and Susan B. Anthony. What am I bid for one of these?" Cathy and Barbara stared as the prices rose from hundreds to thousands. The bundle of old fountain pens averaged three hundred dollars apiece and the hideous picture frame brought $50,000.

"Well, if he thinks I'm going to stand for being ripped off, he's got another think coming!" Barbara stomped over to confront Mr. Atwood.

He listened to her increasingly loud protests and reached into his pocket, bringing out the piece of paper she had hastily written a month ago. "I thought you might show up today. My lawyer says this will stand up in court."

Barbara was speechless.

He continued quietly, "Ordinarily, I wouldn't have allowed someone to dispose of items so hastily. But, you see, I knew Hazel. Your benefactress was a lovely woman who always spoke highly of you. It's too bad you didn't return her affection."

Cathy couldn't bear to look at Barbara, to see the bitter disappointment on her face.

~

Librarian is only one of many interesting non-paying jobs held by ***Audrey Eggers***. So when hearing the advice, "Don't quit your day job," she continued to volunteer, but enjoyed the paychecks that came in from freelance writing. The opportunities to write for *GatorTales* and *Emu Today and Tomorrow* have given her enough exotic animal stories to entertain to the point of boredom any group of friends or dining companions. And her assignments to interview Stillwater businessmen and women for the *Stillwater NewsPress* have given her the chance to ask all the nosy questions that have always burned inside.

~

Everybody's Business

by Audrey Eggers

The steeple bell of the First Baptist Church in Semper, Georgia, tolled eleven times at precisely twelve noon. All around town and in the surrounding countryside the locals knew it was twelve o'clock because that bell was always one hour off from April through October. The old church custodian disapproved of Daylight Savings Time and refused to reset the time just to comply with some bureaucrat's half-baked notion of how to improve on God's own timing.

Volunteer librarian Amanda LaCrosse was new to Semper. She counted the chimes and wrote 11:00 a.m. on Haley Zimmer's checkout slip.

"Due two weeks from today, April 21," she said as Haley stuffed the book in her backpack and ran to catch Kristen Wade.

Amanda turned to watch the giggling girls through the large storefront windows. The library was in the old J.C. Penney building. After the failure of a county bond election, volunteers put together shelves of donated lumber, talked Forrest Tower into providing space in one of his many downtown properties, and gathered books from avid readers who had run out of shelf space at home. Amanda routinely visited Friends of the Library sales to add volumes to their stock.

Bev Binghamton, one of the library's most frequent visitors, walked past without coming in. Amanda thought Bev must have a very pressing appointment, not to even wave or glance in the window at their new display. She had never before failed to give Amanda a welcoming smile.

Pastor Reece and his wife Ellie parked across the street and went into Scivally's Pharmacy. Vivian McAlister and Nancy Brewster, another library volunteer, caught up on the town news and gossip in front of Jan Tilley's Tea Room. And an old man in denim bibbed overalls came out of the empty storefront with a scampering honey blond retriever.

Amanda had volunteered at the library in order to meet her new neighbors when she had first come to Semper in January after forced early retirement at the age of 52. Ten years in Atlanta, Georgia, had convinced her that she did not want to return to Minnesota winters. Nor did she want to fight the traffic and crowded malls of Atlanta. Small town southern life seemed to be the answer.

Business was slow, almost nonexistent, for the next several hours. Amanda spent the time reshelving books, sorting through the donation box and sending out late notices. Nancy Brewster came in to help with the after school rush.

When Amanda glanced toward the jingling bell on the front door, Vivian McAlister's fingers wiggled hello. Eye contact was all the woman needed. She bustled over to whisper the latest in Amanda's ear.

"Did you hear what happened?" Vivian's eyes blinked rapidly to ensure her listener knew the importance of the news. "Forrest Tower was murdered!"

"Oh!" was all Amanda managed.

"His housekeeper found him when she brought in groceries. If she hadn't gone back no one would have known until tomorrow when he failed to show up for the bank board meeting. But she didn't want to keep the milk in her hot car while she drove out to Piedmont's for bedding plants so she took it right in the back door and put it in the refrigerator. She was putting away the rest of his groceries. Did you know he makes her buy his hemorrhoid cream? Anyway she heard the phone ringing and he didn't answer it, so she went into the den to pick it up. It was just one of those telephone sales people so she hung up right away, but when she turned around there he was! He was lying in a pool of blood behind the door. She had even tracked blood on the carpet from the door to the telephone!"

Jan Tilley came across from the tea room, and Vivian rushed off to be the first with details of Forrest Tower's demise. She turned around with one last tidbit of information. "They arrested Bev Binghamton!"

Amanda's knees buckled and she groped for the rickety desk chair behind her.

"But you know Nancy Brewster was pretty mad about her store."

Nancy peered around the mystery shelf to glare at the unrepentant gossip.

Amanda was barely aware of their words or actions. Bev Binghamton arrested! Bev was one of the few people who had really befriended Amanda. They didn't meet for lunch or chatter on the phone, but Bev had cared enough to learn that Amanda had never been married and had no family. She moved over to make room for Amanda at Sunday services. Amanda could not believe that same woman had murdered Forrest Towers.

When Nancy came to the front with an empty book cart Amanda said, "I need to leave just a little early."

Nancy shrugged. "I can handle it as long as Vivian doesn't come back in. You always stay late anyway. Go ahead."

Amanda found Bev pacing the floor at home. She had not been arrested but was one of the prime suspects and had been questioned. Still she managed a weak smile and offered a cup of tea.

"Forrest liked to manage people and his money gave him the means to do it. I'm a suspect because I protested that my son deserved the Semper High Scholarship. It turns out that Forrest not only put up the money for the yearly scholarship but inserted a requirement that he could veto the committee's choice. It nearly always goes to the valedictorian, but in his opinion, I come from poor white trash and therefore the scholarship should go to someone more deserving."

"Vivian implied Nancy Brewster had a motive."

"Forrest did cancel Nancy's lease and forced her out of business. She had a dress shop next door to the pharmacy."

"I don't mean to gossip," said Amanda, "but I know it wasn't you. Who else might have been angry with him?"

"He crossed Rev. Reece in the church council meeting last Tuesday and told him to start looking for another church."

"How could he manage to fire a pastor?"

"His donations have kept that church afloat. If he stopped giving, there was no money for a pastor's salary. And he even caused a lot of trouble for some teenagers. One of the kids worked in Forrest's lumber mill and was letting the others in for some late night keg parties."

"Is there anyone in town who isn't a suspect?"

"Vivian McAlister. She always has an alibi because she goes from one listening ear to the next, dawn to dusk."

"Bev, I just can't believe they really think you killed him. Everyone in town knows you."

"That's the problem in a small town. Whoever the murderer is, we probably all know him."

"I saw you walk past the library today and you seemed – preoccupied."

Bev grabbed Amanda's wrist. "I was on my way to a little bit of Mother's comfort. Meat loaf, mashed potatoes and commiseration." Her grip tightened. "I don't suppose you know what time it was?"

"I do know! It was eleven o'clock. I had just written the time on Haley Zimmer's checkout slip. Does that help?"

The alibi helped and it also cleared the pastor, Nancy Brewster and two of the affected teens.

Then Ellie Reese came into the library and checked out a book on the stroke of three according to the First Baptist Church steeple bell. Ellie chuckled when she saw what Amanda had written on the checkout slip. "Still not used to our church bell, hum?"

Ellie explained about their stubborn church custodian. But it wasn't until eleven the following morning that Amanda realized what had happened to Bev's alibi. Should she tell Bev? Should she call the sheriff? Surely Ellie Reese wouldn't tell anyone, because it was also her husband's alibi.

But Ellie Reese did talk to the sheriff. "Turns out Amanda LaCrosse must have seen us when we picked up that prescription instead of when we dropped it off."

And when they questioned Nancy Brewster again she claimed she and Vivian had stood and talked about her plans for a new dress shop both before and after lunch in

Jan Tilley's Tea Room.

Vivian McAlister was thrilled to corroborate Nancy's story. First hand information was the best of all gossip fodder.

Bev Binghamton was a suspect again. And Amanda began to wonder if she could do anything to really clear her friend. But even Vivian McAlister's gossip failed to provide any information that could clear Bev or implicate the true killer.

On Friday morning Amanda saw the same old man and his dog entering Nancy Brewster's former dress shop. She hurried from the library and hardly checked for traffic before darting across the street.

"Sir! Sir, could I speak with you?"

The old man set a clipboard and measuring tape on a table beside the door and called the dog back to his side with two snaps of his fingers. His hair was almost white, but when he smiled Amanda lowered her age estimate by ten years. He waved her inside.

"I saw you earlier this week, right here, a little later, about noon."

He nodded.

"Maybe you know something that can help my friend. She's accused of killing Forrest Tower."

It turned out Charles Dylan was a contractor in business with his son. Tower had hired them to inspect the building and draw up plans for an antique mall. Charles did not know that Forrest Tower was dead.

"I took a break about ten and had some coffee in the tea room. But I haven't talked to any of the locals since then."

A gruff voice interrupted. "A couple of outsiders are not going to ruin my life." Jan Tilley, in her frilly tea room apron, gestured to the back of the building with a small handgun.

"How'd you get in here?"

"You haven't bothered to inspect the basement. We're connected."

"Well, lady, I do know you got pretty emotional when you found out why I was here." He glanced toward Amanda. "Tower's conversion plans included the tea room. Her lease wasn't going to be renewed."

"I went out the back and over to Tower's house to reason with him. The Tea Room could have a door into this place. Good for business for both of us. He said maybe I'd like a little space in the mall." She mimicked the condescension in Tower's voice. "There's quite a market for those uncomfortable little chairs."

"But you had customers. Nancy Brewster and Vivian McAlister." Amanda immediately covered her mouth with her hand. What was she doing arguing with an armed killer?

"Vivian talks so much she had no idea how long she'd waited to get a menu. They said I looked a little hot, and I just told them I'd been baking."

A sneer lifted one corner of her mouth. "Forrest looked pretty surprised when I pulled out this gun. It stopped an abusive husband, it stopped Forrest Tower, and it's going to stop the two of you."

Amanda's voice shook, but Jan Tilley seemed ready to boast of her accomplishments. "How are you going to conceal two more murders right next door to your own business?"

"I know a few places in the basement of this old building where they won't find you for years."

Bless that old man's heart. Charles clicked his tongue and the dog barked sharply in Jan's direction. When she turned Charles ducked and lunged at Jan Tilley's legs and took her down like a high school line backer. The gun flew out of her hand and slid across the floor to Amanda's feet.

The dog jumped onto her legs while Charles sat on her

back and pushed a lock of white hair off his forehead. Amanda stared at the gun and then took the ever-present pencil from her pocket and picked it up by the trigger guard as she had seen police officers do on "Law and Order."

"If you two can sit on her a little while longer, I'll go call the sheriff."

~

Afterword

by Audrey Eggers

Almost every Oklahoman has an immediate connection to animals – whether it is the memory of gathering eggs with a grandmother, milking cows with a grandfather, riding horseback for work or recreation, sharing a home or barn with cats or dogs, watching birds through a picture window, raising emu: the new livestock, or listening to coyotes howl behind the fence.

Just as The Cozy Crime Writers are familiar with Oklahoma settings and patterns of speech, ***most*** of us naturally include livestock, wild animals and pets into our plots both as characters and as part of the setting.

Mostly we hope you enjoyed these mysteries – ***Almostly Murder…With Pets***.

~

Order More Copies of

Almostly Murder … With Pets

by The Cozy Crime Writers

Deborah Bouziden
M. E. Cooper
Audrey Eggers
Rey Hanan
Marion Moore Hill
Sara Sue Hoklotubbe
Sharon K. Hudgins
Judith Sexton
Moira K. Wiley

Presented by M. E. Cooper and Audrey Eggers

By mail:
Padlock Mystery Press
412 E Ninth
Stillwater, Oklahoma 74074

At your local bookstore:
Request by title and ISBN number: 0-9662020-7-4

On the Internet:
www.mecooper.com

Historical Mystery Titles

from

Padlock Mystery Press

Key Deceptions by M. E. Cooper
ISBN 0-9662020-3-1

Key Confrontations by M. E. Cooper
ISBN 0-9662020-6-6

In 15th century Bologna, Italy, Avisa Baglatoni uses locksmithing skills and courage to save her own life and those she loves.

"M. E. Cooper's fascinating depiction of medieval Italy will delight readers. ***Key Deceptions*** is an intriguing and unusual mystery with appealing characters." Carolyn Hart, author of Death on Demand and Henrie O series.

Uncivil Death by M. E. Cooper
ISBN 0-9662020-4-X

Confederate General W. W. Loring, assisted by his aide, must use all his wits to prevent a grave miscarriage of justice while encamped near Winchester, Virginia in February, 1862.

"M. E. Cooper's characters come forth in such blazing reality that you will see, feel, taste and smell the entire military operation woven into a solid murder mystery. ***Uncivil Death*** is a must read to put on your summer book list."

Dusty Richards, author of *Rancher's Law*, St. Martin's.

True Crime Titles

from

Padlock Mystery Press

Fatal Trust by M. E. Cooper
ISBN 0-9662020-2-3

Medical doctor, Rebecca Johnson, disappeared from the parking lot of Crawford Memorial Hospital in Fort Smith Arkansas. When she vanished, she was known to be carrying $1,500,000 in cash. M. E. Cooper reveals the shocking facts of this tragic murder, including ten pages of photographs.

Unlikely Assassins by M. E. Cooper
ISBN 0-9662020-1-5

The nude bodies of Mark and Delores Stepp were discovered in the bedroom of their home, stabbed and shot. Two unlikely suspects emerged.

"A disturbing account of family woes that led to two of the most vicious murders ever perpetrated in the congenial community of Stillwater, Oklahoma. Mary Ellen Cooper's probe into the puzzling mind of a former honor student will make parents sleep with one eye open." Nina Downey Higgins, co-author of *Devil Child.*